Melissa Senate has written many novels for Mills & Boon and other publishers, including her debut, *See Jane Date*, which was made into a film for TV. She also wrote seven books for Mills & Boon's True Love line under the pen name Meg Maxwell. Her novels have been published in over twenty-five countries. Melissa lives on the coast of Maine with her teenage son; their rescue shepherd mix, Flash; and a lap cat named Cleo. For more information, please visit her website, melissasenate.com.

A Wyoming
Christmas
to Remember

MELISSA SENATE

MILLS & BOON

First published in Great Britain 2019
by Mills & Boon, an imprint of HarperCollins*Publishers*
1 London Bridge Street, London, SE1 9GF

Large Print edition 2019

© 2019 Melissa Senate

ISBN: 978-0-263-08355-2

This book is produced from independently certified
FSC™ paper to ensure responsible forest management. For
more information visit www.harpercollins.co.uk/green.

Printed and bound in Great Britain
by CPI Group (UK) Ltd, Croydon, CR0 4YY

As always, for Max, with love.

Chapter One

"You're my *husband*?" Maddie Wolfe asked.

She tried to latch on to the word, for something, anything, to associate *husband* with the total stranger sitting at her bedside. The stranger holding her hand in both of his and looking at her with worried green eyes.

"My name is Sawyer Wolfe," he said. "We've been married for seven years."

"Sawyer Wolfe. Seven years," she repeated. "And I'm Maddie Wolfe?" She hadn't even known that until he'd told her when she'd woken up just a couple minutes ago with no idea who she was, where she was or who *he* was. Her mind, where her identity and memories should be, was a big blank nothing.

She glanced from him to what was beside her bed—quietly beeping hospital machines, an IV pole. A television mounted on the beige-yellow wall. A long, wide window. A miniature Christmas tree decorated with garland and ornaments on the windowsill and so many poinsettia plants—pink, red, white—she couldn't even count them. There were even more bouquets of flowers.

I'm in a hospital, she realized, reaching up to the goose egg on her forehead and the deep scratch beside it. That would explain why her head felt so woozy and achy. And maybe why her mind was so blank. *I'm…*she thought, trying to come up with her name on her own. *Maddie*

Wolfe? Didn't ring a bell. She tried for her age. Nothing. Where she lived. But there was just that nothingness again.

Sawyer Wolfe nodded, his eyes shimmering with tears, relief, concern. When her own eyes had fluttered open, the first thing she saw was him. He'd jumped up, shouted, "Maddie's awake! My wife is awake!" and then grabbed a white call button attached to her bed and pressed it three times before sitting back down and taking her hand, kissing the back of it over and over.

"Your wife?" she'd asked.

He'd glanced up from the kissing of her hand, clearly confused. "Maddie?"

"Maddie?" she'd repeated, more confused.

He'd sat up very straight. "Maddie, do you know who you are? Who I am?"

She'd looked at him long and hard, and believe you me, he was something to behold. But nothing about this man was familiar.

She'd shaken her head, which had her reaching up to the goose egg, the deep scratch beside it.

"Your name is Maddie Wolfe," he'd told her. "I'm Sawyer Wolfe, your husband. You were in a car crash—it was snowing hard and you hit a guardrail."

Now, before she could ask him anything else, two women came rushing in, one in blue scrubs, the other in a white lab coat with a name tag: Dr. Louisa Addison.

The nurse began taking her vitals: temperature, blood pressure.

"Maddie doesn't seem to know her name or who I am," Sawyer said to the doctor.

Dr. Addison asked her a bunch of questions she didn't know the answers to. *What is your name? What year is it? Who is the president of the United States?*

As the doctor jotted things down on her

chart, Maddie wondered how she knew what a chart was if she didn't know what year it was. She glanced at the four pink poinsettias on the windowsill, clearly knowing what those were. Her gaze moved to the little Christmas tree. There were two Woodstock ornaments—the little yellow bird from *Peanuts*, Snoopy's buddy. Why would she know that but not even know it was Christmastime if the tree hadn't clued her in?

Ow, my head, she thought, letting the questions, the confusing buzz go. The blankness came back, and she instantly felt better.

She glanced at the man—six-two, maybe six-three, dark hair, a scar above his left eyebrow. If she thought he looked worried before, it didn't come close to the concern on his face now.

"My mind is blank," she said to both of them. "Why is my mind blank?" She tried to think what day it was, but as she ran through the days of the week, none registered as the right one. She bolted upright. "Why don't I know my name? Sawyer said I was in a car crash?"

Dr. Addison nodded. "You've sustained a head injury that seems to have affected your memory. But rest assured, you're in good hands. You are Maddie Wolfe, thirty-two years old. Your husband, Sawyer Wolfe, is right here—he's the chief of police in Wedlock Creek. You're in Brewer County Hospital in Wyoming, transferred here from the Wedlock Creek Clinic."

No memory: amnesia. She knew what that was. It explained why her mind was full of holes. She grasped on to what she was told. *My name is Maddie Wolfe. My husband is Sawyer Wolfe. Police chief. Wedlock Creek.*

Nothing. Her own name was unfamiliar. Her husband was a stranger.

She swallowed, glancing over at the

Woodstock ornament. She kept her focus on the little yellow bird, and for some reason, it comforted her.

"Maddie," Dr. Addison said, "Sawyer hasn't left your side in the two days since you were brought in." The doctor offered an encouraging smile to both Maddie and the man. "Your parents and sister were here this morning and said they'd be back this afternoon."

Parents and a sister! She couldn't even remember her own family.

"I'll go text them that you're awake," Sawyer said, leaping up and heading near the door, where he pulled out his phone.

As the doctor typed instructions into a computer monitor against the wall and the nurse checked her IV, Maddie stared at Sawyer. Surely if he were her husband, she would remember something. A familiarity. A flash of their wedding day. The two of them at home. Something, anything.

"Will my memory return?" Maddie asked the doctor.

Dr. Addison turned to her. "Amnesia is a tricky thing. There are a few different kinds, and yours is likely caused by trauma. We'll have to wait and see. I did have a patient a few years ago who'd suffered temporary amnesia from a bad fall. His memory returned to full function within three weeks."

"Three weeks?" she repeated. "I might not remember anything about myself for three weeks?"

Dr. Addison gave her a reassuring smile. "Could be sooner. But we'll run some tests, and based on how well you're doing now, I don't see any reason why you can't be discharged later today."

Discharged where? Where did she live?

With your husband, she reminded herself.

She bolted upright again, her gaze moving to Sawyer, who pocketed his phone and came back over, sitting down and taking her hand in both of his. "Do I— do we—have children?" she asked him. She couldn't forget her own children. She couldn't.

"No," he said, glancing away for a moment. "Your parents and Jenna will be here in fifteen minutes," he said. "They're ecstatic you're awake. I let them know you might not remember them straightaway."

"Jenna?" she asked.

"Your twin sister. You're very close. To your parents too. Your family is incredible—very warm and loving."

That was good.

She took a deep breath and looked at her hand in his. Her left hand. She wasn't wearing a wedding ring. He wore one, though—a gold band. So where was hers?

"Why aren't I wearing a wedding ring?" she asked.

His expression changed on a dime. He

looked at her, then down at his feet. Dark brown cowboy boots.

Uh oh, she thought. *He doesn't want to tell me. What is* that *about?*

Two orderlies came in just then, and Dr. Addison let Maddie know it was time for her CT scan, and that by the time she was done, her family would probably be here.

"I'll be waiting right here," Sawyer said, gently cupping his hand to her cheek.

As the orderlies wheeled her toward the door, she realized she missed Sawyer— looking at him, talking to him, her hand in his, his hand on her face. That had to be a good sign, right?

Even if she wasn't wearing her ring.

Almost exactly the same time that the orderlies wheeled Maddie back into her hospital room, her family arrived. Sawyer had been hoping for some time alone with Maddie, but he'd get that later at home. Right now, her family needed to see her.

The MacLeods—pronounced *Mac-Loud*—all hovered around her bed. They lived up to their name and then some.

"Maddie!" April MacLeod shouted, throwing her arms around her daughter. "Oh goodness, I'm not squeezing any sore spots, am I? Let me look at you. Oh my, that's some goose egg. But that'll go down, lickety-split. We brought you chicken noodle soup from that fancy gourmet place you like in Brewer. You love chicken noodle." She stared at Maddie, then waved her hand in the air. "Did I even tell you who I am? I'm your beloved mother, that's who. You and your sister here are my world. And this guy—" she slung an arm around her tall, gray-haired husband's shoulder "—married thirty-four years next Saturday."

"Glad you're awake, Maddie-girl," Ace MacLeod said, giving his daughter a gentle hug. Tears shone in his blue eyes and he blinked them back. "You scared us half to death."

Jenna MacLeod Spinner leaned down to hug her twin as best she could—her sixth-months-pregnant belly didn't let her get as close as she clearly wanted. "So word is that you don't remember anything. Trust me, we're unforgettable. It'll come back to you."

Maddie gave a shy smile. "I hope so. You definitely seem like people I'd like to know."

April laughed her huge, throaty, I-used-to-smoke laugh. "You adore us. Can't get enough of us. But you take it easy until the doctor says otherwise. I know you'll try to come back to work, and I won't hear of it. Not until you're cleared."

Maddie tilted her head. "Work? What do I do?"

"You manage the family business—MacLeod's Multiples Emporium."

"A multiples emporium?" Maddie repeated. She couldn't even guess what that was.

"Wedlock Creek, our hometown, is famous for its multiples," April explained. "The Wedlock Creek Wedding Chapel has a legend attached to it—for a hundred years now. Those who marry there will have multiples in some way, whether through luck, a little help from science or through marriage."

"Which one are Jenna and me?" Maddie asked with a grin.

"Pure luck," her mom said. "Multiples run on both sides of the family. And since there are so many multiples in town, we started a business devoted to twins and triplets and quads and quints twenty-five years ago. Gift baskets, layettes, baby shower accoutrements, personalized gifts, anything anyone could want to celebrate all things multiples." She glanced at Sawyer, then smiled down at Maddie. "Well,

Maddie-girl, we're going to let you get out of here. Sawyer will take you home, and we'll call later to see how you are."

Maddie gave a quick smile and nod, and it was strange how Sawyer couldn't read her expressions anymore. He knew her so well. But now that she didn't even know how she felt about anything or anyone, all her reactions were new to him.

An hour later, after eating a light lunch and having her vitals checked again, Dr. Addison ran through some instructions, handed over the discharge papers and Maddie was free to leave.

"Earlier I asked your mom to stop by the house and bring you clothes to change into," Sawyer said. "And your favorite boots." He handed her an overnight bag.

"Ah, thank you. I'll just be a bit." She headed into the bathroom with the bag.

Why aren't I wearing my wedding ring?

He hadn't answered that question, and he was sure she was going to ask again.

But he didn't want to tell her. He didn't want to talk about any of that.

He shouldn't be almost glad that she'd forgotten what had made her drive away from him the morning she'd crashed her car. He couldn't take back what he'd said, even if he hadn't meant it, even if he'd said it in anger and frustration. He *had* said it—and Maddie couldn't remember.

He was going to have to tell her the truth.

His phone pinged with a text. His rookie, Justin Mobley.

Hey, Chief. Annie Potterowski's beagle swiped a hot pretzel out of a kid's hand by the chapel earlier, and the parents want to file a formal complaint. Apparently, it's the second time in a month. I'll handle it.

Sawyer texted back.

Just what I like to hear.

Welcome to Wedlock Creek, where food-snatching beagles accounted for half the crime. The other half was the usual— expired car registration, vandalism, the odd burglary, car accidents, teenagers up to old tricks, fights and occasionally more serious issues. Sawyer had lived in Wedlock Creek his entire life, and very little surprised him. Except what had come out of his mouth the morning of Maddie's crash. And the crash itself. And the memory loss.

His wife didn't remember any of it. The past few months and how hard things had been. Maddie grabbing her cool-gel pillow and stomping from their bedroom to the living room to sleep on the sofa. The conversations that always ended in arguments and then stalemates. She didn't remember any of that.

It's like we can have a fresh start, he thought. Unfairly. Because Maddie was who she was and wanted what she wanted.

And she would regain her memory—within a few weeks, if that long. And then what? They would be in exactly the place they were before she'd driven off—and hit the guardrail.

She came out of the bathroom looking more like herself—her beautiful long light brown hair was out if its ponytail, and she'd exchanged the hospital gown for an off-white sweater and jeans. And her favorite footwear, red cowboy boots.

"I stared at myself in the mirror for quite a while," she said with a smile. "I look a lot like my twin. Except for the pregnant belly."

For a moment, a hot surge of panic hit him. He thought she'd regained her memory—and that she'd tell him she wasn't going *anywhere* with him. But he could tell by her warm, open expression that she had no memory of how she and Jenna had always talked of being pregnant at the same time, new mothers together, new aunts to each other's babies together.

She didn't remember any of that.

He slung her bag over his shoulder. "Ready to go?"

"Ready," she said.

This had to be so strange for her. Following him blindly, not recognizing a thing about him or her past or anyone.

He put the bag down and looked directly at her. "Maddie, I want you to know that I love you very much. I've loved you since we were both five years old, and I'll love you when I'm ninety-two. Anything I can do to make you more comfortable, you just say the word, okay?"

He'd caught them both by surprise with that. She stared at him for a moment, then her expression softened. "I appreciate that. And did you say since we were *five* years old?"

"That's how long we've known each

other. My family moved next door to yours."

"That's some history we have," she said. "I wish I could remember it, Sawyer."

"In due time, you will."

Inside his SUV, they buckled up, and he headed for Wedlock Creek, a half hour from Brewer. Maddie asked some questions on the way—if they went to Brewer, a bigger town, often (no); did they have favorite restaurants (yes—Mexican in Brewer and several in Wedlock Creek); what kind of music they liked (Maddie liked her top-forty hits and '70s music, and Sawyer had long been all about the Beatles and had a fondness for country).

Finally, they pulled into town, Maddie staring out the window.

"Wow, this town is so pretty," she said. "All the shops and restaurants decked out for Christmas. Wedlock Creek looks like a postcard. Ooh, look at that," she said, pointing.

Sawyer glanced up at the Wedlock Creek Wedding Chapel, built a hundred years ago. Even on a weekday at 5:17 p.m., there were tourists walking around the grounds, several brides in white gowns, the food trucks and carts at this end of Main Street doing brisk business even on a cold December day. Annie Potterowski, the elderly officiant and caretaker of the chapel along with her husband, was walking the pretzel-stealing beagle, who had a rap sheet for that kind of behavior. Wedlock Creek residents loved the chapel's mascot dog, but his habit of jumping up and swiping food out of people's hands was cute only the first time it happened to someone, then they were less inclined to laugh about it. The beagle was wearing a red-and-green Christmas sweater, and Sawyer had to admit it added to his mischievous charm.

"That's the chapel your mom was telling you about," he said, "with the legend of the multiples." A big green wreath with a red bow was on the arched door, which was dotted with white Christmas lights.

"Did we marry there?"

He nodded. *Please don't ask what I know you're going to ask next*, he thought.

"But no little multiples of our own?"

There it was. "No. Ah, this is us," he rushed to add, turning onto Woods Road. He pulled into the driveway of the last house on the dead-end street, an antique-white arts-and-crafts-style bungalow—or at least that was what she'd called it. To him it was just home.

She stepped out of the car, stopping to stare up at the house. "Wow, we live here? It's gorgeous. And the sparkling Christmas lights around the front trees make it look like an enchanted cottage."

They day he'd hung the lights, they hadn't been speaking. He'd needed something to do, something for her, something for *them*, so he'd spent an hour wrapping the strands around the trees and the porch. Maddie had broken their mutual silent treatment by thanking him. *It's Christmastime*, she'd said. *We've got to get through this so we can have a good Christmas*. But they'd done exactly that for a few Christmases now, and Maddie had sounded so unsure of herself.

"You fell in love with this house when you were a kid," he said now, handing Maddie her set of keys. "It was built in the early 1900s. You saw it on your paper route and said, 'Sawyer, one day, I'm gonna live in this dream house.' And you do."

She smiled, seeming lost in thought for a moment. "How long have we lived here?"

"I bought it for us as a surprise the day I proposed to you," he said. "My offer was accepted on the house, and I raced over to your condo to ask you to marry me. That offer was accepted too." He smiled, remembering how she'd flung herself into his arms, kissing him all over his face, completely forgetting to say yes. In fact, it wasn't until he'd told her he had another surprise for her and driven her over to the house with the Sale Pending sign in front that he reminded her she hadn't. She'd been sobbing happily over the house and unable to speak for ten minutes and finally took his face in her hands and said, "Sawyer, yes. Always yes."

Always yes. Except recently, when there had been so much *no* between them that their history together hadn't been able to protect them.

She took all that in, then glanced at the key chain. "I'm seeing a pattern here. There's a little ceramic Woodstock on here, and there were two ornaments on the little Christmas tree in my hospital room."

"You like birds. And you love Woodstock. Always have. For your birthday every year when we were kids, I would get you something Woodstock. Woodstock erasers, Woodstock socks, Woodstock key chain. In fact, the one in your hand I gave you on your fourteenth birthday."

She smiled. "Really?"

He nodded. "It's freezing out here. Let's head in." He gestured for her to lead the way because he wanted her to feel that this was her house, even if she didn't remember it.

She used her key and opened the door, slowly stepping inside. "I like it!" she exclaimed, nodding at the colorful round area rug in the entryway and vintage Le Chat Noir poster with the black cat on the wall.

"Oh my, who's this?" she asked as a German shepherd hurried up to her with mournful whines. The dog sat at her feet.

"That's Moose, retired K-9. We worked together for years when I was a detective, but for the last three years he's been enjoying a life of leisure. He's eleven years old and adores you."

"Aw," she said, kneeling down to pet him. "Hi, Moose."

"He missed you the past couple of days." *And so did I. Praying you'd wake up. That'd you'd be okay. Bargaining.*

"I'll take your coat," he said, removing his and hanging it up in the hall closet. She unzipped her down jacket and handed it to him, and he hung it up with her red-and-pink scarf, a gift from her knitting-crazy twin.

He watched her walk around the living room, looking at objects and peering at photos. She picked up their wedding photo off the mantel, one of her favorites because that devilish chapel beagle had photobombed him dipping Maddie in a kiss near the steps.

Her shoulders slumped, and she put the photo back. "I can't remember my life."

She shook her head. "And it's clearly a wonderful one. Loving family. Handsome, devoted husband. Lovely home all decked out for Christmas. A sweet dog named Moose." Tears shone in her eyes, and she dropped down onto the sofa, Moose padding over and putting his head on her lap. She leaned over and buried her face in, hugging the dog.

Well, if it makes you feel any better, things weren't all sunshine and roses.

Badumpa. Not.

He sat down beside her, hands on his knees. And before he could even think about it, he blurted out, "It's my fault you got into the accident, Maddie. I said something that upset you, and you got in your car and peeled out fast to get away from me."

She turned to him. "What did you say?"

"That maybe we *should* separate." He closed his eyes for a second and let out a breath. He'd hated saying that. The first time and now.

"The emphasis on *should* makes me think someone else suggested it first. Me?"

He shook his head. "Right before the accident, we'd had our weekly appointment with a mediator slash marriage counselor. We'd been going to her to help us deal with a stalemate. She said it seemed to her that neither of us was willing to budge and that maybe we should think about separating. I got so upset, I stalked out. You followed and we argued outside. And then I said it—maybe we *should* separate."

"What could have possibly come between us to that degree?" she asked.

He took a breath. "Starting a family."

"Ah," she said, looking at her left hand. Her *bare* left hand. "Now things are making sense. Before I got in my car and huffed away, did I yank off my wedding ring because I was angry about that and about you saying maybe we should separate?"

"That's exactly right. You took it off and handed it to me. I have it in my wallet." He'd never forget how that had made him feel, like his entire world was crumbling and he couldn't catch the pieces.

"So I assume it's me who wants kids?" she asked.

He nodded.

"And you're content with things as they are. Wife, dog, job."

He nodded again.

"Married seven years, thirty-two years old, seems like a reasonable time—past reasonable time—to start a family," she said, a prompting lilt in her voice.

Acid churned in his gut. "I never wanted kids. You always did. And you counted on me changing my mind. You had no doubt I would, even though I cautioned you about that. You never really believed deep down that I wouldn't want a 'little Wolfe, a little us'—as you used to say."

She tilted her head. "And you still don't?"

He got up and walked over to the windows, looking out at the snow still clinging to the bare tree limbs. "The past two days, while you were lying in that hospital bed…and I had no idea if you'd wake up… I made so many bargains. If only you'd wake up, I'd agree to ten kids. As many as you wanted."

"So we're going to have ten kids?"

He turned around to face her. "If that's what you want."

"Because you bargained?"

He nodded. "The most important thing to me was having you back. I have that. So yes. Ten kids." He'd almost lost her. He'd said, *prayed*, that he'd give anything to have her back. And he'd meant it.

She stared at him, lifting her chin, and he had no idea what she was thinking. Her expressions, the way her mind worked now—all that was new to him. "Well, the only thing I want right now is my memory back. Maybe just being here, in my home, with you, will jog something, trigger something."

He hoped so. Until then, they had this rare chance to be together without the past stomping on their marriage. He had the unfair advantage of knowing everything about them while she knew nothing, and there was no way he'd take it. He'd always be honest with Maddie. And what was most true this minute was that he loved her more than anything, would do anything for her. Ten children. Twenty.

All that mattered was that she'd survived, that she'd be all right, that she was home.

Chapter Two

Maddie needed to take a big step back, let everything she'd learned settle in her mind, her bones, so she suggested a tour of the house. Sawyer seemed relieved. She followed him upstairs, admiring the photos lining the wall. Pictures of the two of them—together—at so many different ages, from early childhood to what looked like recently. She and Sawyer, age five or six, holding kiddie fishing rods at a riverbank, a bucket between them. She and Sawyer, middle school years, arms linked for a semiformal, Maddie liking her pale pink dress. She and Sawyer, early twenties, Sawyer in a Wedlock Creek Police Department T-shirt, giving Maddie a piggyback ride. A couple with a long history together.

Upstairs was a wide landing with a sitting area. Off it were four rooms. Sawyer opened doors. The first was a guest room. Next to it a large bathroom. And the next room was completely empty.

"Couldn't figure out what to do with the space?" she asked, raising an eyebrow.

"You earmarked it as the nursery," he said, glancing away.

"Ah." She peered into the room—pale gray walls, wood floor, closet, four big windows. It would make a nice nursery—with furnishings in it. She imagined herself walking past this room every day, well aware it was empty. *That must have burned*, she thought. For both of them. A constant reminder of their stalemate.

"And this is our bedroom," he said, opening the door to a big, cozy room, a four-poster bed with a fluffy white down comforter between two windows. There were plump pillows and a table on either side, matching lamps and a book on each—a history of Wyoming and a mystery. She wondered which was her side, her book. *And* what it would be like to slip under that soft, warm comforter beside a man she knew was her husband—and yet didn't know at all. As if he could read her mind, he added, "I can sleep in the guest room or take the couch until your memory returns. I don't want you to feel uncomfortable."

"Well, we don't know what will make my memory return, and since routine might help, I say we do what we always do. You're my husband, and intellectually, I know that, so I'm going with it."

He nodded and, if she wasn't mistaken, looked kind of relieved.

So she would be sleeping beside him tonight. The thought had her taking him in on a purely physical level, and he was so attractive to her that a little burst of excitement and some butterflies let loose in her belly. She liked the way he looked at her with his serious green eyes—as if she were someone very special to him, and despite the issues in their marriage, that did seem clear to her. Plus, her family obviously liked him. And he was tall and strong and the top cop here in Wedlock Creek. Good looks aside, there was something very trustworthy about Sawyer Wolfe.

Of course, Maddie had little to go on in that department. Amnesiac Maddie had known him all of a few hours.

She walked over to a huge closet and opened it. His and hers. Hers on the left. She was very organized. Two piles of sweaters sat next to a row of hung jeans. She had lots of those. She also had a lot of shoes. She moved over to the dresser and opened the top drawer. *Ooh.* Many lacy bras and underwear. Some sexy nighties. A flutter swept her belly again, and she found herself very aware of him sitting on the edge of the bed, watching her.

On top of the dresser was a round mirrored tray holding perfume and a red velvet box. Inside she found jewelry. Earrings, bangle bracelets. A diamond tennis bracelet. Necklaces. A stunning diamond ring, square and surrounded by little baguettes in a gold setting. She thought about her wedding ring inside his wallet. Interesting that he kept it there instead of having put it in here.

She bit her lip and turned around to face him. "I assume asking you why you don't want children, never wanted children, isn't a simple one."

"It is and isn't," he said.

"But after seven years of marriage? A strong marriage?"

"I've always had a lot on my plate," he said, standing up and moving over to the window. He shoved his hands into his pockets. "I've been chief at the WCPD for only almost a year now, and since I got that promotion on the young side, I felt I had to really prove myself. And before that, I *wanted* to be chief and worked double time to earn the job, so the timing just never seemed right to even think about starting a family. I have so much responsibility at work—for the town, for my staff—that I guess I couldn't see having that kind of responsibility at home too. A baby needing more than I could give."

A lot on his plate. A baby needing more than he could give. Both of those sounded like excuses, and she had a feeling the Maddie she'd been before the *thonk* on the head knew the real reasons he didn't want children. The reasons he wasn't mentioning.

"Hungry?" he asked with a tight smile. "I could heat up your mom's chili and corn bread—she brought over a ton of food for me the day of the accident. I could barely choke down coffee, though."

Quite a change of subject. He clearly didn't want to talk about the state of their marriage anymore. "I had the hospital's cream of something soup," she said. "And some stale crackers. So I'm good for a few hours." She glanced outside. "It's a pretty nice day—I wouldn't mind walking into town and visiting my family's store."

He raised an eyebrow. "You feel up to it? Dr. Addison said you shouldn't go overboard trying to get back up to speed or even acclimated."

"I don't feel woozy at all. And my curiosity has the better of me right now." Plus, she wanted to pepper him with questions—about everything—and despite not knowing him at all, she knew from his expression that *he* wasn't up to *that*. "MacLeod's Multiples Emporium isn't far from here, is it?" Their house was just two blocks off the main street with all its charming-looking shops and restaurants.

He shook his head. "Walking distance— it's right on Main Street, a couple minutes' walk from the wedding chapel. You can't miss MacLeod's—there's a painted wood sign with baby stuff on it—crib, baby shoes, baby bottles. And the windows are decorated to the nines for Christmas."

I love Christmas. The thought startled her until she realized it was new knowledge from her response to that adorable miniature tree on her hospital window-sill and the shops decked out and the way their house was decorated for the holidays. She had no doubt she'd always loved Christmas. "I'd like to go check it out. Since I worked there, maybe it'll ring a bell."

"You'll call me or text me if you feel overwhelmed or want to go home?" he asked. "I'll come get you right away."

She nodded, scrolling through her contacts on her phone. "Yup, there you are. Sawyer—cell and work." Her family was in there too. And a bunch of other people whose names she didn't recognize.

"I'll drop you there, then go check in at the station for a bit," he said. "We can meet up when you're ready to go home."

"Sounds good," she said.

They headed back downstairs, and he handed Maddie her down jacket and scarf and put on a heavy brown leather jacket. He stood in front of the door, and Maddie had the feeling he almost didn't want to let her go, that he liked having her in the house, their house. She wondered if he was worried about their marriage, if their impasse had gotten even bigger than their shared history, their love.

And *she* wondered if, when her memory did return, they'd be right back in that snowy moment outside the mediator's office.

According to Sawyer, thirty-eight degrees in Wyoming in December was practically springlike, so they decided to walk the couple of blocks into town. He'd mentioned that the police station was just another half mile down. Wedlock Creek was bustling, people going in and out of stores, carrying bright bags with wrapped gifts poking out. The moment they arrived on the corner of Main Street, they were mobbed by well-wishers.

"It's so wonderful to see you out and about!" one woman said, reaching for Maddie's mittened hand. "We were all so worried. No one more than Sawyer, of course. And maybe your mom and dad."

Sawyer smiled. "You're right, Brenna," he said, making a point of her name.

Maddie caught on quickly that, after

the third such back-and-forth, Sawyer was covering for her lack of memory, and luckily, acquaintances were giving something of a wide berth since she'd gotten out of the hospital only that afternoon. "Do I know *everyone*?" she asked as they finally headed across the street toward MacLeod's Multiples Emporium.

"Yup. Both of us do. Wedlock Creek is a small town, and we've lived here our entire lives. And I'm the chief of police, so everyone knows me. We knew everyone without that added to the mix."

Maddie looked up at the pastel painted sign atop the length of her family's business. A family walked past—with two red-haired identical twin girls. A woman wheeling a triple stroller was across the street. Multiples everywhere. Including right here—*me*, she thought.

"Your dad made the sign and painted it," Sawyer said. "He's quite a craftsman. He hand makes all the furniture

MacLeod's sells, cribs and bassinets and other wood items. He has a big following."

"How wonderful," she said, admiring the sign and the easel out front listing a colorful array of items in someone's excellent handwriting. Everything from personalization to layettes to baby paraphernalia to children's clothing. She watched two women wheeling twin strollers go inside the shop; two more came out carrying big yellow shopping bags with the MacLeod's logo.

"I'll probably be thirty minutes or so," she said to Sawyer. "I'll just visit the store and say hi to my family if they're there. I don't think I'll walk around town just yet on my own in case I run into someone who knows me and I have no idea who they are. Seems so complicated to explain about my memory."

He nodded. "I'll pick you up here in thirty minutes."

She smiled, and he leaned over awkwardly and kissed her on the cheek. He hesitated before pulling back, and she had the feeling he'd wanted to embrace her. More than embrace—hold her, tightly. Frankly, she could use a hug.

"See you in a bit," she said, those flutters in her belly again, and darted into the shop. She turned back to see Sawyer watching her as if to make sure she was okay. She gave a wave and walked in farther. When she looked back, he was finally heading up the street.

The shop was both elegant and folksy at the same time and separated into sections for clothing and furniture and baby paraphernalia. The place was pretty crowded too; Maddie could see two saleswomen with MacLeod's name tags helping shoppers.

"Maddie!"

She turned to find her twin, Jenna, smiling and rushing up to her. She and

Jenna really did look a lot alike. They both had the same blue eyes and slightly long nose, wavy light brown hair past their shoulders. Jenna wore a dark purple maternity wrap dress and gray suede knee-high boots, lots of gold bangles on her arm. And a gold wedding band and solitaire diamond ring.

"I'm surprised to see you," Jenna said, straightening a huge stuffed giraffe. "Feeling all right?"

"I feel pretty good. A little weird not knowing anything about myself—okay, a lot weird. I figured I'd come check out the family business. Do you work here too?"

Jenna nodded. "I'm a saleswoman, and let me tell you, the huge belly helps. Five minutes ago, I sold three personalized cribs—the ones our dad famously hand makes—and then the mom and her mom came back a minute later and added the triple bassinets they were waffling on.

And then the mom bought three of these," she said, pointing to three big stuffed bear chairs with pink or blue bow ties around their necks.

"Ooh, you are good. Did I work on the floor too?"

"Nah, you're more a back-office type. You're not a pushy schmoozer like me."

Maddie laughed. "Speaking of pushy, can I ask you something?"

"Of course."

She leaned a bit closer to whisper. "Was I pushing Sawyer to have a baby?"

Jenna's smile faltered. "Maddie, I love you. You're my sister, my twin. But you don't remember anything about your life, and I'm not sure I should fill in details that are personal between you and your husband."

Maddie thought about that. "I get it. How about details *about* my husband. He said we grew up next door to each other."

"More like Sawyer grew up in our

house. He's been an honorary MacLeod since he was five, when he and his dad moved into the in-law apartment of our neighbors' house. The Wolfe door opened very close to our side porch, so that's how you and Sawyer became such good friends. Apparently I was anti boy, but you adored Sawyer from the get-go."

"He and his dad lived in an in-law apartment? With his dad's in-laws?"

Jenna shook her head. "No. That's just what one- or two-bedroom apartments attached to private homes are called. They were usually meant for parents or in-laws as they aged. The neighbors back then were friendly with Sawyer's mom, so they felt terrible about the situation and gave his dad a big break on rent."

"What situation?" Maddie asked.

A shopper walked up to them. "Excuse me, is it possible to get those adorable little cowboy hats personalized for my impending triplet nephews?"

Jenna nodded at the woman. "Personalization is MacLeod's specialty. I set aside two of those hats for my little babies-to-be—a girl and boy. My husband and I still can't agree on names, so the personalization will have to wait."

The woman laughed. "Names are the one thing my husband and I *do* agree on." She put three impossibly tiny leather cowboy hats in her basket and continued on in the stuffed animal area.

Jenna led Maddie over near the checkout desk away from the shoppers. "Sawyer's mom died from complications after his birth. His dad raised him alone. Well, he tried, I guess. But he really wasn't cut out for fatherhood. I think the landlords let him stay to make sure Sawyer would have a safe place to live next to caring neighbors. They were traveling a lot, but between them and us looking out for Sawyer, he had what he needed."

Maddie frowned. "Sounds rough."

"I'm sure it was. No mom. A father who wasn't really present—and lots of girlfriends in and out. To be honest, if he hadn't lived next door to us and slept over so often, there's a good chance he would have been taken away and put in the foster-care system. His father was that neglectful. But no one wanted to see that happen."

Maddie thought about how Sawyer had said he'd always known he hadn't wanted kids. That made a little more sense to her now.

She imagined a little Sawyer, three, five, eight, ten. No mother. A father with issues. Alone, hungry, no guidance. Slipping next door to the warm, welcoming MacLeods. She was glad her family had been there for him. That *she'd* been there for him. They'd been best friends their whole lives.

She could *also* imagine wanting to start a family. Being thirty-two and the ole biological clock ticking away. "I must have figured he'd change his mind about wanting kids," Maddie said. "But he never did, huh?"

Jenna bit her lip and seemed unsure if she should say anything. "No. This is all secondhand from you, so I guess it's okay for me to tell you." She shook her head. "How crazy is this situation? Anyway, yes. In fact, he put off proposing because of it. Because he knew you wanted a houseful of kids, and he just wanted you and a good dog."

"But he did propose. He told me he bought my dream house and then proposed."

Jenna smiled. "He asked Mom and Dad what to do. He told them he loved you more than anything, but he didn't want kids and you did, and how could he propose when he couldn't promise the one thing you really wanted. They said he'd change his mind. *I* said he'd change his mind. *You* said he'd change his mind. And finally, Sawyer got to a place where he could *imagine* changing his mind— one day. Maybe. I think because he loved you so much he could imagine it, you know, even if he didn't want it for himself. You told me he made it very clear he couldn't promise he'd ever want kids and that there was a very good chance he wouldn't."

Yikes. "I feel awful," Maddie said, tears stinging the backs of her eyes. "He was so honest about it. It's not fair to him."

"And it's not fair to you either, Maddie," Jenna said gently. "You were both always honest with each other. But suddenly time stopped being on your side. And let me tell you, having a pregnant twin sister didn't help."

Maddie eyed her twin's big, lovely belly. "I bet." She sucked in a breath. "All I want now is my memory back. My life back. I don't even remember wanting a baby. I don't really know what that would even *feel* like."

"Well, maybe you and Sawyer can use this time to get to know each other all over again without that stalemate pressing on you. It's always been there the past few years, worse this past year. But now the two of you can just be Maddie and Sawyer again. For a time anyway."

Maddie nodded. "Because my memory will come back. Dr. Addison said it could be a week, three weeks, possibly longer, but she thinks just a few weeks."

"It'll all come back. With these new memories you're making every moment now."

"Do you think we were headed for a separation?" Maddie asked.

Jenna frowned. "I can't even imagine

it. You were class BFFs every year since first grade. You were MadSaw—your own celebrity nickname. You guys love each other."

"He said he made all kinds of bargains while I was unconscious. That if I woke up, he'd give me ten kids."

"He told you that?" Jenna asked, touching a hand to her heart.

Maddie nodded. "That's not how I want to start my family off. I'd want to have a baby with a man who wanted that baby. Not because of a harrowing bargain he made skyward."

"Oh, Maddie. It's complicated, right? Just get to know your husband during this time. You'll be getting to know yourself too. You're still you."

"Excuse me?" a very pregnant woman said. "Do you make programmable lullaby players? My husband is a budding country singer, and we want a player that has those stars-and-moons lights for the ceiling while playing my husband singing."

"Absolutely," Jenna said. "I just ordered my version of that. Little cows jumping over the moon to the tune of lullabies sung by one of my favorite singers. Let me show you our catalog."

The woman's face lit up. Suddenly Maddie realized that she may have been more a back-office type because all the moms-to-be buying such fun stuff must have made Maddie feel very left out.

The door jangled and there was Sawyer. Maddie wrapped her sister in a hug. "Thank you," she whispered. "You helped a lot."

Jenna hugged her back and waved at Sawyer. "I'm always here for you."

Maddie smiled and left Jenna to her customer. Suddenly she felt a lot better and a little heavyhearted about what was to come.

But as she walked over to Sawyer, the

handsome, green-eyed man in the brown leather jacket, she wanted to wrap her arms around him—tight. That much she knew for sure.

Chapter Three

They walked home from town, Maddie linking her arm through his, which buoyed him like nothing else. There was affection in that gesture, a degree of trust, and that meant a great deal to him since he'd lost that over the past several months. Once, for a very long time, she'd believed he'd never hurt her. Then he'd started outwardly denying her what she wanted most. And the bond began fraying.

Now, in the simplest way, he felt her saying yes to him, to *them*.

"How about lasagna for dinner?" he asked. "Your mother really did stock the freezer after your accident. She said all that cooking gave her something to do with her mind and hands or she'd have gone nuts. There are five containers of lasagna alone."

Then again, Sawyer thought he should be doing more for Maddie than just heating up her very kind mother's bounty of food. But April MacLeod was a great cook and he a mediocre one, and she'd made their favorites. Lasagna. Shepherd's pie. Fettuccini carbonara. Her amazing chili and three pans of corn bread, which Sawyer could polish off in one sitting. He felt like he should be cooking for her, figuring out how to make some of her favorite dishes, such as blackened salmon, without burning it, and risotto.

"Do I love lasagna?" she asked.

"It's only your very favorite food on earth. Mine too. We used to make it as teenagers. I did a layer, you did a layer and then we'd stuff our faces."

She smiled. "What else do I love?"

"Blackened everything. Also, fish tacos. Caesar salad. Cheeseburgers. The Pie Diner's chili potpie. Your mother's brisket. Coffee chip ice cream."

"What don't I like?" she asked. "In general, I mean."

"That you can't figure out yoga. You don't like corn. You don't like horror movies."

She smiled. "What did I do when I wasn't working?"

"Well, the past few months you started volunteering for the town's Holiday Happymakers program. You devoted quite a few hours a day to it."

"Holiday Happymakers? What's that?"

"A group that plans ways the town can help those who can't afford Christmas or can't do much in the way of celebrating because of illness or other issues. You started an adopt-a-family program to provide holiday decorations and gifts for each family member. Anyone can leave a letter on the Christmas tree in the community center with a wish list for the family or a relative."

"I sound kind!" she said. "Glad to hear it."

"You are. Very."

"What was Christmas like when you were growing up?" she asked.

He frowned at the thought. "I spent every Christmas at your house. My dad didn't always have his act together, or he disappeared to a girlfriend's. Your parents always hung a stocking for me—stuffed it too. And there were always presents for me under the tree. I got them gifts, too, and always wished I could have afforded better than a scented candle for your parents. But that's what I got them every year."

"Aw," she said. "I'll bet they loved it."

"Your mom always made a show of sniffing it and lighting it and setting it right on the mantel." He'd never forget her mother's kindness. Ever.

"My sister told me the basics of your childhood," she said. "I hope that's all right. She figured because it was something we all knew, it wasn't telling tales or talking about your personal business, which she refused to do."

"I don't mind your family filling in holes," he said. "The truth is the truth. And I'm not interested in hiding anything from you. Our marriage was rocky two days ago when you got into the accident and months before that. Very rocky."

"I'm glad I don't remember," she said, tears poking again. "I guess that's wrong. But all I know is that I'm not unhappy or sad or anxious or wanting anything. I don't know who I am, but I feel safe because of you and the MacLeods. So if

I'm in limbo, at least it's a nice limbo. A Christmas limbo, at that."

He smiled. "That's a nice way to look at it."

She tightened her hold on his arm, and again he felt like they had a chance. Even if it was just this limbo chance. This Christmas limbo chance. Right now, she was his again.

At the house, Sawyer let out Moose, who raced around the yard, which still held a good covering of snow. Maddie threw his favorite squeaky ball at least twenty times, and he chased it over and over, dropping it by her foot.

"Sorry, Moose, I think my arm is going to give out," she said, kneeling down to give the German shepherd a rub and a pat.

The phone was ringing, so they headed inside, Moose going over to his big red fluffy dog bed by the fireplace in the living room. They missed the call, and about twenty others, from Maddie's parents and sister, checking in, and friends and fellow volunteers on the Holiday Happymakers committee.

"That's really nice," Maddie said after she listened to all the messages.

Sawyer nodded. "Everyone likes you. Well, I'm gonna go get dinner ready. Want a glass of wine?"

"I have a craving for a little eggnog. Do we have any?"

"Of course. You love eggnog." He was back in half a minute with two glasses of eggnog. He handed her one, then clinked hers.

"Yum," she said. "You don't want help with dinner?"

"My job is reheating," he said. "So no. You relax. It'll be ready in fifteen minutes, per your mother's very specific instructions."

She flashed him a smile and sank onto the couch, Moose coming over and sitting in front of her, his head on her knee. Sawyer watched her give the dog a warm hug, wanting more than anything to pull her into his arms and hold her. But he was afraid to overwhelm her, and he had a feeling he should let her make any physical moves.

Over dinner they talked more about what they liked and didn't, laughing more in twenty minutes than they had in the past three months. After dinner and cleaning up the kitchen together, they bundled up and took Moose on a long walk around the neighborhood, enjoying the holiday lights. Back home they watched a singing competition on TV, Maddie sitting very close beside him on the couch as she drank a little more eggnog. Then she yawned—twice—and they realized she'd better get to bed. It had been a long day for her, busier than either expected it'd be once she was discharged, and she could probably use the rest.

He followed her up the stairs, Moose trailing them. In their bedroom, she poked around her dresser drawers and pulled out blue flannel pj bottoms with little Woodstocks all over and a long-sleeved pink T-shirt.

"So... I'll just change in the bathroom," she said. "Is that weird?"

"Not at all. We just met this morning."

She laughed. "It really does feel that way."

It did feel that way. And not—at the same time. All their history was front and center in his head and heart, weighing heavily. He was taking a T-shirt and pair of sweats from the dresser when she came out of the bathroom. Her hair was pulled back into a low ponytail so her goose egg was even more prominent, the scratch beside it too.

"Which side of the bed is mine?" she asked.

"Window side. I'm the door side."

"Ah," she said, "so the robbers get you first."

He smiled. "Exactly. And so I can roll out of bed and rush out if an emergency call comes in."

She picked up the mystery on her bedside table and looked at the cover. "Am I reading this?"

"I think you just plucked it off the bookcase to pick up whenever I'd come in the bedroom—to avoid talking," he said. "When you weren't pretending to be sleeping."

"Yeesh. That bad, huh?"

He looked at his wife, his beautiful Maddie, wishing he could say otherwise. "Yeah. There were recent moments, though, that even our stalemate couldn't ruin. When I plugged in the Christmas tree for the first time. When Moose ate a stick that required a trip to the vet, and we were both so worried about him that we actually held hands in the vet's office for the first time in forever."

"Was Moose okay?" she asked, sitting on the edge of the bed and turning toward him.

"Yeah."

"But we weren't. We're not," she amended. "I'm not sure I want to remember that, Sawyer."

"Well, like I said, I'm prepared to give you ten kids. So, once your memory is back, we're all set. We'll start a family."

She frowned. "But, Sawyer, you don't want a baby. You're only agreeing because you made a spiritual pact."

"But I meant it. I'm prepared to have a baby."

"Well, that's not what Maddie-who-I-don't-remember would want. That Maddie would want you to *want* to have a baby, a family of your own."

He let out a breath, exhausted. "I don't

know that there should be conditions. A yes is a yes, right?"

"No. The yes was about something else. Having your wife back. Giving her what she wanted so badly because you made a bargain with the heavens. It's not actually about what you want, Sawyer."

"So what you're saying is that I can't win?" That came out sharper than he intended. They weren't supposed to be arguing. Maddie needed her head to settle; she needed rest. Not this. He turned away, barely able to take it—that they were back in this place, arguing.

"I don't know," she said. "I don't really know anything, do I?"

Dammit. He walked over to her side of the bed where she was sitting, and he held out his arms. She bit her lip and looked up at him, then stood and walked right into his embrace. He wrapped his arms around her, resting his head atop hers, and hell if he didn't feel tears stinging his eyes. "I'm just so grateful you're alive, Maddie. That we have a second chance. That's the truest thing I know."

She raised her head and looked at him, then kissed him on the lips, just a peck, but a kiss nonetheless. Then she got into bed and drew the down comforter up to her neck.

He slipped in beside her knowing there was no way he'd get a wink of sleep tonight.

Maddie's eyes fluttered open as she felt Sawyer suddenly bolt up beside her. She heard the doorbell ring—twice. Then a third time.

She sat up and glanced at her phone on her bedside table. It was 12:19 a.m.

"Someone's at the door?" she asked.

His phone pinged, and he grabbed it, reading the screen. "Oh man."

"What?"

"It's my brother. He's the one ringing

the bell." He texted something back, then got out of bed. "I'll handle this. Try to go back to bed, Maddie. You need your sleep."

Sawyer had a brother? No one mentioned a brother.

There was no way she was going back to bed. Sawyer's brother was at the door after midnight, pounding on the ringer and texting? Something was definitely up.

She found a terry bathrobe on a hook in the bathroom and put it on, then tiptoed out of the bedroom and down the stairs to the bottom step as Sawyer reached the door. Unless she was mistaken, he took a breath before pulling open the door.

Standing there, hands jammed into the pockets of his jeans, was a younger version of Sawyer, with shaggier and lighter hair. He wore a black leather bomber jacket and a thick black ski hat. He had an overnight bag slung over his shoulder.

Before he could say a word, Sawyer barked, "Cole, it's really late. And Maddie's not feeling well."

"Yeah, hello to you," Cole said.

Sawyer didn't invite him in. "The last time you needed a place to crash and I let you stay a couple days, you robbed us blind and disappeared. If you need a place to stay, I'll front you some money I know I'll never see again, but you can't stay here."

"I'm not looking to stay here," Cole said, his body language all fidgety and nervous. "Um, look, it's not good for the twins to be out in the cold so long, okay?"

"What?" Sawyer asked. "What twins?"

Cole leaned down and picked something up out of view. Sawyer stepped onto the porch and Maddie heard his gasp. She rushed toward the door as Cole came inside carrying two infant car seats, a baby asleep in each one.

Sawyer stared at the babies, shutting the

door behind him. "What the hell is going on? Whose babies are these?"

Cole put the car seats down on the foyer rug, then dropped the bag off his shoulder, rubbing his face with both hands. He looked absolutely miserable. And nervous.

Maddie stepped out of the shadows. "Hi."

"Hey, Maddie." Cole nodded at her, his expression warmer, and she had the feeling they'd gotten along at some point or that she'd been kind to him. "Whoa, what happened to you? That's some bump on your forehead."

"Car accident," she said. "I'm okay, though."

He nodded and reached out to squeeze her hand. Yup, she'd been right. They had definitely gotten along—or just better than Cole and his brother did.

"What the hell, Cole?" Sawyer barked. "Whose babies are these?"

"I got an ex pregnant," he answered, his voice shaky. "We got back together, but then I was fired from my job, and she told me forget it and hooked up with someone else, but he said no way is he gonna be a father. So she went into labor yesterday and called me and I rushed over. I witnessed the birth—wow, that was something." He shook his head. "And I thought maybe my ex would say she wanted us to have a second chance, but she told me she wasn't ready for motherhood and didn't want the twins. She even signed away her parental rights. Unless I accepted responsibility for them, the state would have put them up for adoption."

This time Maddie gasped. She looked down at the two infants—newborns—asleep in the carriers.

"Good Lord," Sawyer said, shaking his head.

Cole closed his eyes for a second, his expression pained. "I stood outside the hospital nursery, staring through the glass at their bassinets and holding the forms to give up my rights so they could be placed for adoption. A nurse saw me struggling, I guess. She came over and told me that allowing them to be placed for adoption could be the best thing I could do for them if I couldn't take care of them. She said it was up to me, that I was their father. Damn that word, Sawyer. Father. Father. Father." His eyes brimmed with tears, and he slashed a hand underneath and sucked in a breath.

Sawyer put a hand on his brother's shoulder, his expression full of so many emotions Maddie couldn't begin to pick them out.

"But I couldn't sign, Sawyer," Cole continued. "I couldn't just abandon them completely like that. I know what it's like to be tossed aside."

Maddie's chest constricted. She had no idea what Cole's story was—and from what she knew, he wasn't raised with Sawyer next door to the MacLeods, or his name would have come up. But whatever his story was, it certainly didn't sound good.

Cole dropped down on the bottom step of the staircase, covering his face with his hands, then stood up and paced. "My name is on the application for the birth certificate that Gigi started filling out—and they look like me, I can see that, even though I thought all babies just looked like babies. They're mine. But I can't take care of them. I can't take care of myself."

"Jesus, Cole," Sawyer said, his gaze moving from his brother to the infants.

"The twins were cleared to leave, and the nurses told me what to buy before I could leave with them—two infant car seats. She also told me to buy some newborn-sized pajamas. When I returned with all that, they gave me a starter pack of diapers and formula and other stuff I'd need. I sat in my car in the hospital parking lot for a half hour with the twins in the back seat and completely panicked, no clue what to do, what to think, how I was gonna do this. Then I drove here."

"Did you name them?" Maddie asked gently.

Cole didn't respond; he just ran a hand through his hair. He looked so frantic. "I'm gonna get their other bag from my car. Be right back."

He dashed out, closing the door behind him. Sawyer stared at Maddie, then looked at the two sleeping infants in the carriers again. They looked so peaceful, blissfully unaware of all that had happened since they came into the world just a day ago. All that was going on now.

Maddie heard a car start and peel away, tires screeching.

Sawyer raced to the door and flung it open, rushing out to the porch. Maddie followed, pulling her bathrobe tighter around her in the cold December night air.

She saw the car's red taillights barely pause at the stop sign up on Main Street before turning right. Maddie recalled the sign for the freeway in that direction. "He's not coming back tonight, is he?" she said. More a statement than a question.

Sawyer took her hand and led her inside, closing and locking the door behind them. He stared at the babies, then at her. "I'm not sure he's *ever* coming back."

Chapter Four

For a moment, Sawyer just stood staring at the two babies on the floor in their blue car seats. But then one of them opened his eyes, and Sawyer almost jumped.

The little slate-blue eyes opened a bit wider, the baby moving slightly, his bow lips quirking.

"That one's awake!" Maddie said, stepping over. She picked up the carrier and looked at Sawyer until he picked up the other carrier. His brain was not quite catching up just yet. As a cop, as the chief of police, he never had time to be shocked. Police work, training, protocol always took over. But right now, where his brother was concerned, where his newborn nephews were concerned, shock had permeated. There were few people in this world who could get to him. Cole was one of them.

He followed Maddie into the living room. She set the carrier on the rug and began unlatching the harness, the baby staring at her, the bow lips still quirking.

"Oh my goodness, look at you," she said, her voice holding a wonder he hadn't heard in a long time. She moved aside the white-and-blue-striped blanket covering the baby, slid a hand behind the baby's neck and another under his bottom, gently lifting him from the seat. "Aren't you just beautiful," she whispered, rocking the infant slightly in her arms.

Sawyer eyed the baby. He looked healthy, good color in his cheeks, eyes clear. He wore plush green pajamas with feet. Thank heavens for that kind nurse, telling Cole what to buy, giving him a little breathing room to leave and return.

He could imagine Cole driving from the hospital with the twins, no idea where he was going, what he was doing. And then the idea lighting in his mind: Sawyer and Maddie.

The baby in Maddie's arms began to squirm some. *You're my nephew*, Sawyer thought, trying to wrap his mind around that. *I'm someone's uncle. Two someones.*

"Hey, there's what looks like an *M* on his cap—in marker," Maddie said, peering closer. "*M* for *male*?"

Sawyer looked at the other baby's cap. "This one has an *S* on it. Could be their initials." He froze, then looked at Maddie. "*M* and *S*? That's us. Maddie and Sawyer."

Her eyes widened. "Coincidence?"

He shrugged, barely able to take in everything, let alone begin to process and think straight.

"Could you root around the overnight bag and see if the starter kit of bottles and formula are inside?" she asked. "He doesn't feel wet, but he's probably hungry. Babies eat every few hours the first couple of months, I think."

He picked up the bag Cole had left behind and sat down with it, going through it. Yup, luckily there were the hospital-issued beginner supplies. A small pack of newborn-sized diapers. Two bottles and a few different nipples. Pacifiers. Formula. Two blankets, a few extra baby hats. Enough to get through the night.

And some clipped-together paperwork. The birth certificate applications. Cole *had* named them. One was Shane Wolfe. The other was Max Wolfe. Something told him the nurse had initialed their caps as a just-in-case.

"Their names are Shane and Max,"

he said, holding up the application. He flipped through the papers. The relinquishment of Gigi Andersen's parental rights, signed by two witnesses, both nurses. He shook his head.

"Shane and Max. Sawyer and Maddie. That *can't* be coincidence."

"I'll go make up a bottle," he said, unable to wrap his mind around that. "At the PD, we've watched training videos on assisting with births and newborn care, so none of this is all that unfamiliar to me."

And honestly, he was grateful for the chance to slip away into the kitchen so that he could catch his breath. *Take* a breath. He scanned the directions on the small canister of formula, then added the powder and water to the bottle, shook it up and put on the correct nipple. He quickly made up the other bottle just in case the little guy's brother woke up.

Cries coming from the living room— two different voices—indicated he had.

Sawyer rushed back in, bottles in hand, and gave one to Maddie.

As he reached in to pick up the other baby, he glanced over at Maddie, leaning back against the sofa, feeding the infant, her expression so serene, so full of marvel. *This is what she always wanted*, he thought. *All she wanted.*

His chest squeezed and he focused on the other baby, gently lifting him out and settling beside Maddie with the other bottle.

Man, was this weird. *You're my nephew*, he thought, watching the baby slurping the bottle quite contentedly, his blue eyes opening and closing as if he couldn't decide whether or not he wanted to be awake or asleep again. The baby was his kin, but nothing about this felt natural. Maybe because he and Cole had been estranged for the past couple of years. There had been times over the years when Sawyer had felt close to Cole no matter the distance between them, physical or emotional. But since that last time, when Sawyer had given Cole a place to crash for a few days and he'd stolen cash and a diamond bracelet that Maddie had inherited from her late grandmother, Sawyer's heart had closed up to his brother. He'd felt done with Cole, the last straw.

And now this.

With the newborn cradled in her arms, Maddie reached into the bag and rooted around and pulled out a folded-up mat. "I think this little one needs a change."

She lay the baby down on the mat and undid his wet diaper. She found a small container of cornstarch and gave his bottom a sprinkle, then found some rubbing alcohol and cotton pads and gently cleaned the umbilical cord area before putting on a fresh diaper. "I have no idea how I know how to do all this. Either instinct or common sense."

Or you wanted to be a mother for so

*long and did so much research in prep-
aration that it's in your blood and bones
and veins if not your memory.*

Once the infant in Cole's arms was done
with his bottle, Maddie reached over for
him as well and got him all changed, then
they each sat on the sofa, just holding the
twins, unable to even speak for a time.

"I guess we'll hang on to the paperwork
for a few days," he said. "See if Cole returns." He looked down at the baby in
his arms, *S* for *Shane* and possibly *Sawyer*, then at baby Max in Maddie's arms,
M for *Maddie*. Their mother had signed
away her rights. Their father had taken
off. And here were Maddie and Sawyer, caring for them, all of a day old, for
God knew how long. "I guess it's fitting
they're named after us. *If* they even are."

"Wow—we've got newborn twins to
take care of." She stared down at Max,
then glanced at Sawyer. She seemed

about to say something, but then didn't. "Sawyer?"

He looked at her, shifting Shane in his arms just a bit. The baby didn't even stir.

"Are you okay with this?" she asked. "I mean, taking care of the babies. Given... how you feel about having babies in the first place."

"I do what needs to be done," he said, then regretted it when he noticed the look on her face. A little disappointment, a little surprise, a little *Jeez, really?* "And they're my nephews," he added fast, "so of course I'm okay with it."

The disappointment, surprise and *Jeez, really?* didn't abate with that added pronouncement.

He was striking out here. "Look, Maddie, the most important thing in the world to me fifteen minutes ago was you and only you. You were just in a bad accident. You lost your memory. Taking care of you was my sole priority. Suddenly, we have two newborns added into the mix and no idea what's what."

She took that in, her expression softening a bit. "What's what meaning…"

"Meaning Cole is a wild card. He could come back sobbing in the morning, saying he was just scared and lost his mind and begging us to help him figure out how to do this, be a dad to the babies."

"And of course we'll help."

He nodded. "We will. I'd never turn my back on Cole. I might not invite him to stay here because of what he pulled last time, but I'd never turn my back on him."

"Something about robbing us blind," she said. "Are you and Cole half brothers? You didn't grow up together, from what I can tell."

"We share a father. His mother was a weekend fling, apparently. My dad barely acknowledged Cole—or his mother. If it wasn't for the family resemblance, Hank

Wolfe probably wouldn't have accepted him at all."

Maddie shook her head. "Awful. I guess you didn't see him much growing up."

"His mother never brought him around to our place since she didn't trust Hank. I certainly don't blame her. And every now and again, when my dad wanted to get rid of me, he'd drop me off at Cole's apartment two towns over. His mother wasn't thrilled at having another mouth to feed or kid to watch, so she'd always take me back home in a couple hours."

She shook her head again. "I guess you never had the opportunity to get close."

"Nope. And to make matters worse, Cole thought I had it better because at least I got to live with my dad, not that I had a mother ever. He resented that. I tried to tell him our dad wasn't exactly father of the year, but you know how kids can be about that. Grass is always greener."

"But it sounds like you care about Cole," she said, tilting her head.

"Of course I do. I always felt a kinship with him, always wished we could be closer. I tried for a while, but I could never really trust him. He lies too easily. Takes advantage of people. He got into some trouble with petty stuff a couple years ago and suddenly wanted me to make it go away. That caused a rift when I wouldn't. It's one of the reasons I let him stay the last time, even though I wasn't comfortable. To try to get a relationship back. Then he stole five hundred bucks in cash from an envelope in a kitchen drawer that I'd put there for a contractor, and he stole a bracelet your late grandmother gave you." He hung his head back. "I kind of wish I hadn't told you that, since you had the good fortune of not remembering."

"My grandmother's bracelet?"

"A diamond bracelet you always admired. She left it to you. And he took it. I got it back from the pawn shop, but paying for it infuriated me. Man, was I pissed as hell."

"I'll bet. Sorry, Sawyer. All that sounds really hard."

He nodded. "He'll always be my kid brother, though, you know? Despite, despite, despite. And I consider myself a pretty good judge of people and know a liar when I see and hear one, and I have to say, all that angst and pacing and panic from Cole a little while ago seemed authentic to me. This is new—the babies, I mean. Cole has walked away from family, people, jobs—but walking away from his own children, that clearly triggered a lot for him."

"So you think he'll be back," she said. "Before you said you weren't sure he'd ever come back."

He let out a breath, then looked down at the beautiful baby sleeping in his arms.

"I guess the more I talk it out for myself, the more I realize I don't know. At first, I thought—Cole is gone. That the babies are just too much. But talking about his upbringing just now, what it meant for him to be ignored by our dad. I don't know. Maybe he'll figure some stuff out and come back for his children."

"Meaning I'd better not get too attached."

He froze, staring at her. "You were thinking this would be permanent?"

She gave a little shrug. "I guess either way, it's okay for me to get attached. Either I'll be raising these guys with you or we'll be aunt and uncle."

"Possibly aunt and uncle from a distance," he said, realizing he had to caution her. "Cole could return tomorrow and disappear with these two. And I'll have no recourse. They're his."

"Well, he brought them here for a reason. Even if he needs a night to get his head together, he knows we'll take good care of them. And if he does come back for them, I can't see him taking them far from a soft place for them to land."

"Maybe so," he said. "Speculation has never been my thing, though, Maddie. I'm more wait and see and operate on facts. Like I said, Cole is a wild card."

So yeah—definitely don't get too attached to these guys, he wanted to say. But he could see she was already bonded, after just an hour.

We'll see what the morning brings, he told himself.

"The extra good news is that MacLeod's Multiples Emporium has everything we could possibly need for these two," she said. "I saw that for myself yesterday."

Something told him they'd be taking a trip over there tomorrow and buying up the place, not that the MacLeods would accept a penny.

He *didn't* think Cole would be coming

back. Not tomorrow and not next week. And the longer it got, the longer he'd stay away, because that was how it worked. Not so much out sight, out of mind, but out of sight, out of heart, even if Cole had to force it. One day it would feel too late to come back, and he'd convince himself the babies were better off with Sawyer and Maddie.

But here he was, speculating, when he just said he didn't do that. He had no idea what was in Cole's mind, Cole's heart. He just knew his brother *had* a heart. And that was what worried him and made things better at the same time.

At first Sawyer didn't know what he was hearing. Sounded like a baby crying.

He bolted upright. His nephews.

He glanced at the alarm clock. 4:34 a.m. *Ah, babies. Classic.* He looked over at Maddie, fast asleep. *Good.* She needed to rest.

Sawyer gently peeled back the comforter and padded over to where the babies were lying in their car seats on the carpet across from the end of their bed. They'd slept a nice stretch, so the carriers must be comfortable enough. He picked up Max, who was half crying, half squirming, and the baby instantly quieted down.

"What's the matter, guy?" he whispered. "Hungry? Wet? Just need some company?"

The diaper didn't feel particularly wet, but he changed Max anyway on the mat on the carpet, then put him back in the carrier to bring him downstairs to make up a bottle.

Once he had the bottle ready, he settled on the sofa, Max guzzling away. He heard a cry from upstairs and started to get up, but he could see Maddie on the top step, holding Shane.

"I was hoping you'd sleep through the night," he called up to her. "I was about to go get him."

"I like having babies to take care of," she said, coming down the stairs. "The second I woke up when I realized he was crying, I felt a crazy excitement about rushing out of bed to get him. I must have really wanted a baby, huh."

Yeah. You did. "I guess it's a novelty for now," he said. Again, immediately regretting the words coming out of his mouth. "Cole might be back in a few hours."

Was he cautioning her against getting attached again or doing some serious wishful thinking that his brother would return for his children? Did he want Cole Wolfe walking in and then out with these two precious beings? Cole, who couldn't take care of himself? As his brother himself had said?

Sawyer let out a sigh.

Maddie went into the kitchen to fix a bottle, returning and sitting next to him. "And I guess you really didn't want a baby. *Don't*, I should say."

Shane started fussing and kicking his little legs. Maddie held him upright against her, giving his back some gentle taps, and a big burp came out of that tiny body.

"That feels better, huh," she cooed, cradling the infant in her arms as she continued feeding him.

"My sister told me I've wanted to be a mother since I was really young, that I was always asking to play mommy and baby with our dolls and stuffed animals."

He smiled as a memory came over him. "You used to try to get me to play daddy. I remember you had this demonic-looking baby doll you particularly loved, and I'd run and hide whenever I saw you with it."

She laughed. "I'll bet."

"When we were around ten, you used to say you wanted four kids, two sets of twins, because you loved being a twin. And I used to say I only wanted dogs."

"You knew even back then you didn't want a family?" she asked.

"I knew I always wanted *you* in my life. And a dog. That's it. And when you started really pressing me about starting a family a few years ago, I guess I started retreating without even realizing it. I hated disappointing you, hated denying you something so important to you, but the thought of having a child of my own made me go absolutely cold inside. And I couldn't seem to budge from it."

"Even though our marriage was strong?"

He nodded. "It's not about us or the marriage. It's about me."

Even though she didn't remember any of this, he felt terrible for the Maddie she'd been a few days ago. Loving her husband so much, wanting a child so much. And Sawyer not wanting a child with the same vehemence.

Moose came padding down the stairs. He gave Shane a sniff, then Max, and then lay down at Sawyer's feet. "I used to tell you that Moose was our fur baby. You didn't like that one bit."

"No doubt," she said, setting the almost-empty bottle down. She looked at the German shepherd. "No offense, Moose."

The dog eyed her and put his chin on her foot. "He loved you from the very first day he met you."

She smiled, leaning down to give the dog a scratch behind his ear. "So what do we do now? I guess newborns don't play, do they?"

"Well, I'd like to get them checked out by a pediatrician. I know they just came from the hospital and Cole said they were cleared and discharged, but just for my own peace of mind. Then I think we just walk around with them, talk to them and take care of their every need and want."

"That's the life," she said, giving Shane a little rock.

He looked down at the baby in his arms. Once, he'd promised to take care of *Maddie's* every need and want, and he'd denied her so much. He'd denied her *this*.

But as he shifted Max upright to burp him, that same vague, abstract feeling of terror mixed with *they're not mine, they're not mine* lodged in his gut, as it had when he'd tried to fall asleep last night. Other people always seemed to go to mush around babies, even six-foot-five, two-hundred-twenty-pound Officer Mobley. He'd never heard anyone ooh and aah and then play five rounds of peekaboo like Mobley. But when Sawyer held a baby, all he felt was that dread—and the sure knowledge that the baby belonged to someone else, someone who'd come for him or her.

Except this time.

Chapter Five

Noon came and went, the "deadline" Sawyer had set for his brother to return. Sawyer had called in a favor to a pediatrician he knew in town and had the twins squeezed in for a check-up while Maddie stayed home just in case Cole came back. The good news was that the twins were definitely healthy. The bad news: Cole hadn't called, texted or shown his face at the house.

And so Sawyer and Maddie put the trip to MacLeod's on today's schedule, to buy everything the babies needed. Maddie figured they'd need all the baby paraphernalia on hand no matter what, whether they were looking after the babies or if Cole *did* come back and would bring them by to visit in the typical scenario.

The more she said that kind of thing out loud, the deeper the frown lines on Sawyer's forehead got. Her way, which she was very slowly getting to know, seemed to be to pounce—to ask about everything, including every raised eyebrow of Sawyer's. She was an asker, and she supposed that was good. You didn't ask, you didn't find out anything.

"Why does that make you…unsettled, Sawyer?" she'd inquired just ten minutes ago as they'd settled the twins back in their carriers after feeding them.

"Well, because either way is not exactly what I had planned. For now or the next eighteen years."

"Life is like that, though. You certainly didn't plan for me to lose my memory. Stuff happens, Sawyer."

"With help," he'd said. "Stuff doesn't just happen. I got you angry and you drove off—boom, accident. Cole is reckless—boom, twin newborns who are now in our custody."

"Is that how you look at it? Like the babies are in your custody? À la police custody?"

The frown lines appeared again. "I just don't know what's going to happen, Maddie. And yes, *that* unsettles me."

When he was like that, when he was sort of vulnerably honest, she would feel herself softening and relenting and wanting to give him a hug. But something also told her that Sawyer Wolfe needed a good push. And boy, was he getting one.

After their conversation, he'd gone to make a pot of coffee, and she'd called MacLeod's to let her family know she and

Sawyer would be coming by with their newborn nephews and needed to buy out the joint. Her mother had gasped with joy and said, "Don't you move a muscle! We'll bring everything you need to you! Oh, I can't wait to meet those little Mac-Leod multiples!"

Forty-five minutes later, the pink-and-blue delivery truck arrived, the Mac-Leod's Multiples Emporium logo with its six illustrations of infants in diapers unmistakable. As Sawyer went out to thank them profusely and bring everything in with the help of her dad and a delivery guy, Maddie's mother and sister rushed in to see the newest little members of their family.

"They've got Sawyer's eyes!" April MacLeod said, reaching in to gently take Shane out of his carrier. "Yup, those are definitely Sawyer's eyes—look at the almond shape. I'll bet they turn green by the time these two are three months." She sat down on the living room sofa, gazing at the baby with pure love and devotion.

Maddie pictured Cole Wolfe, eyes so similar to his brother's. Last night, his eyes had been full of pain and panic. She wondered where he was right now. Hours across the country? Twenty minutes away in a motel? Or maybe he was just home, wherever that was. She felt for him, she really did, and she was glad that he could rest assured the babies would be well taken care of by their aunt and uncle.

"And there's just something in the expression," Jenna added, reaching in for Max and carefully cradling him in her arms. The infant gazed up at her with curious slate-blue eyes. "Aw, he's precious. They're both so stinkin' cute."

"So what does this make me?" April asked. "Grandmother-in-law?"

Jenna grinned. "I don't think that's a thing. Or maybe it is. Let's make it a thing so I can be the aunt-in-law."

"I didn't even know Sawyer had a brother," Maddie whispered.

"Oh gosh, that's right," Jenna said, leaning back and shifting the baby in her arms. "They've never been close. You tried over the years to invite Cole to holidays and family events. Sometimes he'd show. He'd stick by your side and avoid Sawyer most of the time."

Poor Sawyer. He'd made it clear he'd always wanted a relationship with his half brother. But the more she got to know Sawyer Wolfe, who was truly as brand-new to her as anyone, the more she realized he probably did the pushing away more than he realized. As he and her father and the delivery guy finished unloading the truck and brought mostly everything upstairs, Maddie heard bits and pieces of Sawyer telling her dad about the situation, talking openly. *He trusts my dad*, she realized. Of course he did; the man practically raised him.

She could see that Sawyer was comfortable and open with Ace MacLeod, and despite the fact that she couldn't remember her own relationship with her parents, she was deeply touched to see that Sawyer clearly felt very close to them.

Within fifteen minutes, the empty room upstairs had been transformed into a nursery. Two rocking bassinets, a cozy pale yellow glider, a dresser–changing table stocked with everything the twins could need, from diapers to cornstarch to chafing ointment, a lullaby player, a big pile of pajamas and caps, blankets and burp cloths. Shane and Max were now fast asleep in their bassinets.

Maddie watched the twins sleep in the sweet little nursery, but as she looked over at Sawyer, she couldn't help noticing that the frown lines were back.

With the baby twins surrounded by the MacLeod clan, Sawyer had made an excuse to leave for just a little while, to take the deep breath he'd barely managed all night. He'd needed some time and space to think—to process what had happened overnight, and so he'd let Maddie know he had to go into work for an hour or two. He put on his uniform, stopped at Java Jane's for a strong, hot cup of coffee and then headed to the Wedlock Creek Chapel, to finally have that talk with elderly caretaker Annie Potterowski about her delinquent dog.

"Annie, you've got to keep Champ on a shorter leash," Sawyer told her. "He's swiped food from people six times this month. Twice from the same kid." This morning, he'd gotten an earful on his voice mail from the parent of Danny Peterman, who thought that children should be able to walk down the street in peace with their allowance-purchased hot pretzel without a dog grabbing it and swallowing it in one mouthful. Apparently, Danny had found it hilarious the first time. Not so much the second time. Especially because Annie had flat-out refused to buy the kid another pretzel.

Short, stout, gray-haired Annie threw her hands up in the air and very slowly bent down to faux-admonish the beagle at her side in the small chapel office.

Normally, he'd leave such small potatoes to his rookie, but Annie was a character (as was her husband and fellow officiant-caretaker), and Mobley had tried too hard to be respectful to eighty-three-year-old Annie, an institution herself in Wedlock Creek, and she'd run roughshod all over him. Besides, Sawyer really had needed a little break from home. From the babies. From this crazy situation he found himself in.

His wife didn't remember him or their life.

He was suddenly taking care of two

newborns who might or might not be sticking around.

Nothing was sure in this world. He knew that. But such uncertainty left him feeling off balance. He didn't like off balance.

"Chief, I told Champ no more swiping—you heard me tell him. And yes, I'll put him on a shorter leash."

Oh, I'm sure Champ was listening. Not. "Thank you, Annie. And if you see someone coming with food in their hand, you might shorten the leash around your hand even more so Champ can't jump and get it. Also, offering to reimburse what Champ steals from people would be the right thing to do."

"One time I offered, someone actually took me up on it!" she huffed.

"Annie Potterowski," he said in his I'm-the-chief-of-police tone.

"Oh, fine, I will, I will, jeez. So what's

this I hear about you and Maddie taking in your baby nephews?"

Word sure spread fast in a small town. "My brother's babies."

"I'm so glad for you and Maddie. Everyone felt so bad," she added on a reverent whisper.

"Bad about what?" he asked. Small town or not, he didn't have the sense Maddie was telling anyone besides her family about their marital troubles.

"You know, your *fertility* issues," she said, whispering the word *fertility*.

Oh, brother. "Why on earth would you think I had fertility issues?"

"You or Maddie. One of you. Otherwise, you'd have three kids by now."

Ah.

"Well, now you have those two little newborns to care for," she said.

"It's not permanent, Annie." It wasn't. It couldn't be.

"Well, for however long. You'll make one heck of a dad, Chief."

He almost choked on his coffee. "What? Me? Why on earth would you say that?"

"You have all the hallmarks of a dad. Dependable. Responsible. Everyone can count on you."

Was that true, though? Maddie hadn't been able to depend on him for the one thing she wanted most out of life: a baby.

"And you're just a good guy," Annie continued. "Kind. Say what you mean and mean what you say. Good sense of humor. Fair-minded. I like you, and I've stopped liking most people. Some of the people I marry in this chapel—I could write a book."

He smiled. "I'm sure."

A knock came at the door. A couple— woman in a wedding gown and veil, man in a tux and a cowboy hat.

"We'd like to get married this minute," the woman said.

"Well, you've come to the right place," Annie said. "Guess you'll need to skedaddle, Chief."

"Got my eye on you, Annie Potterowski," he said, then flashed her a smile. He bent down to give Champ a pat. "You behave yourself, beagle."

As he walked down the long aisle of the beautiful chapel, he easily remembered his own wedding here seven years ago. Maddie had asked him a few times if he was sure he was comfortable marrying at the chapel despite the legend of the multiples. Saying *I do* at the chapel meant not just one baby but two or more. Some might say it was hocus-pocus nonsense, but this town was chock-full of twins and triplets and a few sets of quadruplets. There were even two sets of quints in one family, albeit with quite an age gap.

But Sawyer had known that it meant a lot to Maddie to marry in the century-old chapel, and he'd figured *they* were in control of family planning, not the legend, so the legend itself didn't scare him. Seven years later, no kids, right?

Unless he counted the two in the brand-new nursery of his house.

Those who marry in the chapel will have multiples in some way, shape or form, whether through biology, luck, marriage or happenstance...

He supposed his way was happenstance. Huh.

You'll make one heck of a dad, Chief...

He wasn't too sure about that. He knew he'd do what was needed; that wasn't the problem.

He'd never been able to put the problem into words—that was the real problem, according to Maddie. Or maybe the issue was that he didn't want to put it into words, to dredge up all uncomfortable feelings. His earliest memories included the MacLeods welcoming him at all hours, all holidays, always making a place for him at the table with an "Oh, Sawyer-boy, so glad you're joining us for breakfast—we're having omelets to order." He knew what a good, solid family could be, could mean. He'd grown up witnessing it next door. But his earliest memories also included the ones he'd never been able to shake, the ones that were just there, deep inside him. Times when he couldn't wake up his dad. When he was so hungry for breakfast and the MacLeods weren't home and there wasn't any milk for cereal or bread that wasn't half-green. When a strange woman would tell him to scram for a couple of hours, his dad smiling at her while running his fingers through her hair.

When he was a bit older, twelve, thirteen and so on, all that hadn't mattered so much. He'd gotten used to it and had his own money from his paper route. But family, *his* family, those were the memories lodged in his chest, the ones that had the grip on him. He'd explained all this to Maddie many times, but it didn't make sense to her, and it didn't really make sense to him. The feeling where paternal instincts might be was just dead, didn't exist. He'd never wanted to go there. And he'd avoided it as long as he could.

For a long time, their love had won out, had been stronger. Maddie had truly believed he'd change his mind, and though he'd never promised her that or even said there was a real possibility of it, he'd hoped he would change his mind. That was why he'd felt okay about marrying her with such a fundamental issue standing in their way. The hope had been enough, and Maddie had never doubted he would change his mind.

He'd never changed his mind.

He walked the half mile down to the police station, the bright sun helping with the cold temperature. As he passed the community center, an easel out front next to a decorated Christmas tree caught his attention. *Be a Holiday Happymaker! Adopt a family for the holidays!*

That was the program that Maddie had volunteered for. He headed inside and found a few people plucking envelopes off another big Christmas tree. A sign on the wall read: *Pick an envelope and inside you'll find the holiday wish list for an anonymous family in need. Each family member is to receive at least the item noted on the form. Once complete, drop off the unwrapped items in a bag and include the ticket inside your envelope so that we can match the family with the gifts. Thank you for being a Holiday Happymaker!*

Sawyer plucked an envelope off the tree and opened it.

Anonymous Family #7
Thank you for being our Santa. We

can barely afford heat this winter, let alone gifts. We sure do appreciate this.

Father: Age 26. Heavyweight wool socks for outdoor work (I'm in construction).

Mother: Age 25. A Christmas Eve ham to serve 4. Thank you.

Son: Age 3. A yellow dump truck.

Son: Age 16 months. Warm pajamas with feet.

Sawyer's heart clenched. The mother's Christmas wish for herself was a ham enough to serve her family? The father wanted socks? To wear at his outdoor job?

Done. All done. And then some. *Family number 7, you'll be getting a lot more than socks and ham and pajamas and a dump truck.*

He was about to pluck another envelope when his cell pinged with a text. Reed Barelli, one of his detectives, wanted to talk over a case. He sent back a quick

See you in two minutes, and headed out, turning back to look at the tree. There were so many envelopes that his heart hurt. *Maddie did this*, he thought as he headed into the cold December air. This was her baby, her idea, and she made it happen.

She was such a good person and deserved every bit of happiness. And what she wanted most of all was a family—something he'd denied for so long. He didn't want children; that hadn't changed. But right now, they *had* children—for how long, he didn't know—and while they were here he was going to change his attitude, somehow, someway.

Because hadn't he promised Maddie ten children if that was what she wanted?

Maddie loved the hours she'd spent with the twins and her parents so much that she barely thought about her lack of memory. Her twin had had plans with her husband's family, so she'd had to leave, and the past three hours Maddie and her mom and dad had set up the whole house, stashing "newborn twin survival totes" in all areas so that she—or Sawyer—would never be caught without easy access to a diaper or a burp cloth. April MacLeod had raised twins and was full of tips and tricks for needing more than two hands. By the time her parents had left, Maddie could honestly say she adored the Mac-Leods, even if she couldn't remember them past yesterday.

She stood in the nursery, admiring the pretty yellow glider and round shag rug, the mobiles with pastel little stuffed animals that spun around above the matching white spindle bassinets, the beautiful babies asleep inside them, on soft sheets.

"It's way too quiet in this house for newborn twins."

Maddie whirled around. Sawyer was back. She hadn't even heard him come in, likely because he was trying to be quiet for the babies' sake.

"They're asleep?" he asked, peering past her into each bassinet.

She nodded. "They've been asleep for five minutes, but I've just been standing here watching them, their tiny chests going up and down. It's the most beautiful thing I've ever seen."

He stood beside her, looking down at them, Max in his new tiny-monkey-print pajamas, Shane in his green-and-white-striped ones. "No text or call back from Cole. Not even to ask about them or to check in." He shook his head.

"I suppose he knows how they're doing if they're with us," she said, putting a hand on his arm.

He looked at her. "True. It would be nice to be able to count on him the way he can count on us."

Maddie tilted her head, taking that in. With that simple sentence, everything about Sawyer Wolfe made sense to her. He'd never been able to count on his own family. He'd never had a mother. His father had neglected his well-being. His brother never considered Sawyer's feelings or position. Family friends and good neighbors or not, Sawyer had learned from the most tender of ages that family meant sorrow, loss, worry, fear. No wonder it was so ingrained him not to want to create his *own* family.

She was beginning to understand him, to know him. Maddie had a feeling that the wife she'd been, with all her memories intact, understood Sawyer quite well too—so well that she'd waited and waited and waited for the change of mind she believed he'd come around to. And now she also understood why she'd believed. Because Sawyer's not wanting children wasn't so much a choice he'd made but a feeling he'd been saddled with. She'd been trying to show him what love and family commitment was. But seven years later, at thirty-two, watching her twin sister's belly grow every day, working in a shop full of expectant parents, living in a town where many children were its claim to fame, Maddie could see why she had begun to lose patience with her husband.

"Thank you for taking care of them all day," he said. "I'll take the night shift."

"I loved today," she said. "One peep out of them tonight, and I'm there. I won't be able to stop myself."

"Well, I'll beat you to it."

She smiled and put her hand on his arm again, and he turned toward her. She wanted to open her arms to him, hold him, be held, but she suddenly felt shy. *Because you've known him all of two days*, she reminded herself.

She moved behind him and rubbed his shoulders, needing, wanting to touch him. He stiffened for just a second, then relaxed, dropping his head forward and backward. His muscles were amazing. She itched to slip her hands underneath his shirt.

Turn me around. Kiss me.

"I'll go start dinner," he said instead. "I stopped at the market for your favorite kind of fish, and I'll make it with that Spanish rice you love so much. Sound good?"

Oh, Sawyer. You love me. That is not in question. She moved in front of him and stood just an inch from him, her hands on his chest. "That sounds really good."

He stared at her for a few seconds, then covered one of her hands with his. He stepped back with something of an awkward smile, then almost seemed about to step closer toward her. Moose appeared in the doorway, sitting down and watching them. "Someone else wants dinner too. I'll let you know when ours is ready."

He squeezed her hand and then left the room, Moose padding after him.

Thanks, Moose, she thought, shaking her head with a rueful grin. She was pretty sure Sawyer had been about to kiss her.

Wishful thinking—probably. Maddie did think he wanted to kiss her, but something was holding him back. Their pre-accident issues? She'd have to make it clear she wanted him to kiss her. Hey, they were husband and wife.

Three hours later, dinner done—and delicious—the kitchen cleaned up, the babies fed, changed, read to while Sawyer held both cradled along the length of his arms in the glider, and now once again sleeping in the nursery, Maddie let out a big yawn.

"Tired, huh?" he asked, grabbing a water bottle from the refrigerator.

"Very. I'm definitely ready for bed." *Hint. Hint hint.*

"Why don't you head up, then. I've got some paperwork to catch up on. And as

I said, I've got the twins tonight. You go get that much-needed sleep."

Humph. She wanted him beside her.

"Sawyer, to be honest, I don't feel like being alone."

He froze for a second. "Well, in that case, the paperwork can wait. I'll just, uh, lock up. See you upstairs in a few."

She smiled. *Ask and you shall receive, right?* Sometimes, but right now, it had worked.

She could wait for him to lock up. But she had a feeling her husband was trying to allow her to once again change for bed in privacy.

In their room, she grabbed yoga pants and a long-sleeved T-shirt and went into the bathroom to change. She washed up, then stared at herself in the mirror. Fresh-scrubbed face, long hair back in pony-tail, teeth minty, blue T-shirt. Not exactly sexy.

When she came out of the bathroom,

Sawyer was rooting around in his dresser. He turned and kind of froze, staring at her.

"What?" she asked. "Do I have something in my teeth? Underwear hanging out the back of my yoga pants?"

"You just look beautiful," he said. "You always do."

Maddie smiled. "Even with this half bump and scratch down my forehead?"

His face kind of fell, and Maddie realized she was talking from nerves, rambling away. But what she'd done was remind Sawyer of her accident. *Just take a compliment when it's offered*, she yelled at herself.

She got into bed, tucking the comforter under her arms. The bed was king-size but suddenly felt small. Last night she'd been aware of Sawyer getting into bed beside her, but she'd fallen asleep so darn quickly only to be woken up just an hour later by the doorbell ringing, and she'd barely slept since. Her eyes felt heavy now, but she was more interested in Sawyer than sleep.

He stretched out beside her, turning onto his side to face her. *That* was unexpected. She did the same.

"I adopted a family from the Holiday Happymakers tree," he said. "The dad only wants socks. Warm wool socks. The mother asked for a ham big enough to serve four. I'll be tripling everything and adding things."

She smiled. "That's very kind, Sawyer. This is the program I volunteered for?"

"It was your idea last Christmas. And a very good one."

"Tomorrow, I'd like to pick a family or two to adopt."

"I want to adopt another," he said, "so we can head over in the morning."

She reached out her hand and touched his face, soft and slightly stubbled at the same time. Then she wiggled closer and lifted her face.

He cupped her face with his hands and kissed her, a real kiss, but then he moved back a bit. "Maddie, I want you so much. Trust me when I say that sex has never been an issue between us. But the Maddie you were days ago slept on the sofa the previous two nights. You were upset and angry at me." He hesitated for a second. "I was trying to get out of going to the mediation appointment."

"Why?"

"We weren't getting anywhere. And I hated talking about our problems with a stranger. She was good at getting us to open up, me included, and I hated that."

Maddie smiled. "I see."

"I don't want to take advantage of your loss of memory. And touching you when you're not yourself feels wrong."

Her smile faded.

I want *you to touch me. Oh, flip,* she

thought—was she being fair to herself? To the Maddie Wolfe she couldn't remember? "You want to know what I'm thinking?"

Surprise lit his face. "Yes."

"I'm thinking I want you to touch me. But you're right, Sawyer. I want you to touch me because I *don't* remember. And maybe if I did, I'd be bopping you over the head with the pillow."

"Oh, I think that's way too playful for how you felt those last couple of days, Maddie."

"Really?"

Now it was sadness that crossed his features. "Yeah. I was letting you down. In a very big way. And I couldn't see a way out of that without saying yes to something that I couldn't fathom. I'd think of a baby in our house, and my throat would close up."

"I didn't realize it was that bad."

"I'm not prone to panic, Maddie, but

when I would sit with myself in the dark in the middle of the night, knowing the wife I loved so much was downstairs, miserable and angry and hurting and that it was my fault, I'd think, well, maybe we could just do it, have a baby. And then a rush of cold panic would start in my gut and threaten to drown me. That's how it felt."

Tears pricked the backs of her eyes. "You *didn't* want a baby as much as I *did* want one. Oh God, Sawyer."

"It seems like a no-brainer to everyone. A sweet, darling baby, made of the two of us—what could be more special, more unifying? It's very hard for people to understand."

"Did *I* understand? At all?"

He reached out to move a strand of hair from her face. "Yes. But you really did believe the strength of our marriage would show me, change me, and it didn't."

"Is it awful for you to have Shane and Max here?"

"No," he said. "But I think that's because they're not mine. And they're not permanent. At least I think they're not."

"Maybe *they'll* change your mind."

He held her gaze, his green eyes tender now. "Maybe, Maddie." But he didn't sound sure. Not at all.

She, however, *was* sure of something. Why she'd fallen in love with him, despite that big whopper between them. She was falling in love with him now, could feel her heart moving and quaking and leaning toward him.

He was being true to her—the real her—by not touching her. She wondered if she *was* being anti-Maddie by allowing herself to fall in love all over again with a man saying no to what she wanted so badly. Or saying yes just because he'd pleaded for her life and his prayers had been answered.

She could imagine how many nights she'd lain here rationalizing that she loved him more than anything—more than her desire to have children, to be a mother, and that thought, that knowledge had allowed her to sleep and go on to the next day with him. Until she couldn't take it anymore because she thought his reasons for not wanting children were irrational. She figured anyway.

And now she lay here beside her husband, unable to remember any of it. All she felt was a surge of tenderness for Sawyer, a strong physical attraction and a yearning to be closer to him, in all ways.

"We'll figure it out," she said, touching his cheek.

He gave her rueful smile. "That's what *I* used to say."

"Well, we will." She yawned, her eyes getting heavy, and she turned around, curling against him. She felt him freeze for a second and couldn't help smiling at how predictable he was, deeply satisfied when he wrapped a strong arm around her and probably closed his eyes too.

Chapter Six

Another morning arrived with no text or call from Cole. As Sawyer sat at the kitchen table with Maddie, he stared out the window at the snow dotting the trees, then back at his cell phone lying beside his mug of coffee. He kept expecting it to ring or ping with Cole's number. It never did.

"Where do you think he is?" Maddie asked, giving Shane his bottle.

Sawyer adjusted Max in his arms, tilting up the bottle a bit higher. "You read-ing my mind?"

She smiled. "Just the way you were looking out the window, then down at Max. I just had the feeling you were thinking about your brother."

He eyed her, then put down the almost-empty bottle and took a long drink of his strong coffee. How did she know him so well when she didn't even know her-self right now? Which made him real-ize something else. "I wish I could say I knew him well enough to know where he might be, but I don't. He could be right here in town, hiding out in a motel. He could be clear across Wyoming."

"He looked so upset, though, Sawyer. I can't imagine him just leaving and never coming back. In my current state, I don't know him at all, but from the way he seemed the night he left the twins with us…"

"I know. He was shaken. But people get

shaken and they panic and they do crazy things. I see it all the time."

"Is that what happened to your dad?" she asked.

He stared at her. "My dad?" Talking about his dad was his least favorite subject.

"Your mom died right after you were born. That had to have shaken up your father."

He pictured Hank Wolfe. Tall, muscular, tattoos on each arm, working out with the free weights on the padded bench in his bedroom, a bottle of beer on the floor at the ready. He'd inherited his father's wavy dark hair and green eyes, just as Cole had. "I'm sure it did. He didn't talk much about her, and both sets of grandparents died before I was born, so there's no one to ask about their relationship."

"Alone with a baby, grieving. That had to have taken its toll."

He nodded, his chest feeling tight.

"Well, these guys are fed. Why don't I get them changed, and we can head out to the community center for the Holiday Happymakers tree."

She set down the bottle, now with just a trickle left, then brought Shane against her and gently patted his back. "Change of subject. Okay."

"It's not my favorite one, Maddie."

"Well, turns out you're *not* so lucky I don't remember anything because it means I have to ask you questions. Otherwise, I'd be in the dark. And I hate being in the dark."

"Understood," he said. She was absolutely right. But he still didn't want to talk about his father.

In a half hour, the babies were changed and in their heavy winter fleece buntings, ready to go in the double stroller the Mac-Leods had brought over yesterday. They were all practically out the door when the phone rang—the landline. It was Jenna.

Her husband had taken the day off to accompany Jenna to her ultrasound appointment, and they both had baby twins on the brain and wanted to babysit Shane and Max for a few hours as practice, since they'd have their own baby twins in a few months. Sawyer had to admit he liked the idea of having some time alone with his wife; their nephews had arrived that first night she'd come home from the hospital, and their lives hadn't been their own since.

Ten minutes later, the babies and everything that Jenna and her husband could need for a few hours were now in her sister's house. As he and Maddie walked back to his car, he kept feeling like he was missing something.

"I've been without Shane and Max for all of twenty seconds this morning and I keep having these mini panic attacks that I forgot them somewhere."

"I know what you mean," she said. "We

had them intensely for over twenty-four hours, and suddenly, we're on our own."

"I'm glad about that, Maddie. I think we could use a little time together."

She took his hand and held it. He was surprised by just how good that felt. "So how about we go to the community center to the Holiday Happymakers tree, and then maybe you can show me around. Places that are important to us, important to me."

"Like a 'This is your life, Maddie Wolfe'?"

"Exactly. Dr. Addison said you never know what might trigger my memory to return. It could happen just like that," she added on a snap of her fingers.

And with it, your burning resentment of me, he thought—unfairly. He loved the way things were between them right now. Light. Happy. All good things shining in her eyes when she looked at him. It had been so damned long since she'd looked at him that way.

He drove to town and parked in the lot near the chapel. As they walked toward the nearby community center, so many people out and about shopping for gifts stopped to ask Maddie how she was doing. That she had temporary amnesia was being kept on the down low, so again Sawyer quietly filled in who was who, allowing Maddie to know how to respond. Maddie did a lot for the town, volunteering to lend a hand in many capacities, and the outpouring of well wishes when word had spread about her accident had touched him. He'd gotten so many calls and texts, and the cards and flowers sent to Maddie at the hospital had meant a lot.

As they entered the community center, the small line for the Holiday Happymakers tree was moving quickly. Some people plucked and read and put back the envelope if they didn't like what was inside. Others just took an envelope and left with it.

"Not many envelopes left," Maddie noted. "That's great."

He nodded. "I wouldn't be surprised if people took more than one envelope—like I'm about to do."

"Warms my heart," she said.

Finally they reached the tree. He took off another envelope, and Maddie took two, then they headed over to the benches by the door. They sat and opened their envelopes.

"Aw," Maddie said. "Listen to this. 'I'm eight years old, and all I want for Christmas is a stuffed puppy. I want him to be brown and white like the puppy my neighbor has. My parents say we can't have a dog right now. If you get me a stuffed puppy, I promise to take good care of him. From Stevie.' Aww, so much for anonymous. So cute." She put the form back in the envelope and tucked it into her tote bag. "Let's get her a real puppy!" Maddie said.

Sawyer's eyes practically bugged out of his head. "You're kidding, right?"

Maddie laughed. "Yes. Can you imagine?"

"No, definitely not," he said.

As she opened her second envelope, Sawyer opened his.

Here's my list. Tesla Roadster (red). Round-trip tickets for two to Paris the last two week of August. At least $250 in a gift certificate to Lizabett's Italian Ristorante. $500 in cash. Air Jordan Retro sneakers, size 12.5. Hey, you gotta think big, right? Merry Christmas!

Sawyer rolled his eyes, tucked the list back into the envelope and walked over to the tree to clip it back on. It was the only one of two left now, and he had a feeling it would be opened and returned many times till Christmas. He took the other one and opened it.

I'm not getting anything for Christmas because my father only cares about his stupid new wife and always-crying new baby. I could use a bike so I don't have to ask him for rides anywhere. Whatever. This is just fake Santa. I'm sure I won't be getting anything.
—Jake Russtower.

The kid forgot to keep it anonymous. Russtower. He knew that name. He'd have to check his records, but he was pretty sure he'd come across that name. And not in a good way. He had a feeling the tone and the name combined kept the envelope being opened and put back on the tree. He sighed inwardly and slipped the envelope inside his pocket.

"How was your second one?" he asked.

"A teacher at the middle school asking for books for her classroom," Maddie said. "I'm all over that."

He smiled. "Mine's a little heavier. Looks like some family issues. Kid wanting a bike."

"Well, that kid is lucky you're his secret Santa, then." She wrapped her arm around his, and for the moment, all thoughts went out of his head and everything was right with the world.

Even if everything was as upside down as it got.

"Ready for 'This is your life, Maddie Wolfe'?"

"I'm ready," she said.

They headed out, Maddie putting her gloves on and tightening her scarf. He knew just where to start on the Maddie Wolfe life tour. He just hoped it didn't torpedo him.

* * *

After a call to Maddie's sister and husband to check on the twins, who were "adorable and a pleasure to babysit." Sawyer drove Maddie to Beacon Road. As he pulled up in front of the white house, his gaze was drawn to the house next door, the side porch that was the entrance to the apartment where he grew up. He wanted to drive away.

"Ooh, what's this?" she asked. "Where we grew up?"

"Yup," he said, getting out. As he came around the SUV, she got out too. "The white house was yours. Your parents sold it about seven years ago. You and Jenna moved out and shared an apartment while you were commuting to Wyoming Western University, and then you both got married, so April and Ace decided to downsize and move closer to town and the store."

Maddie peered up at the house. "I was

hoping it would spark something, but nope. Doesn't look the least bit familiar." Her face fell. "I grew up here. I should remember. All my memories are gone. Everything I've been is gone." She turned away, shoving her mittened hands into her coat pockets.

He could kick himself for not realizing she might feel bad about not remembering her own life. Of course she would. Inside, everything might be shiny and new, but she didn't know anyone, didn't recognize anyone, didn't have a single memory beyond the past few days.

"Hey," he said gently, putting an arm around her. "I could fill you in. That was the plan."

She looked up at him. "I guess you'd know. From the very beginning too."

"I do. I've always been there. Well, since we were five."

"Where'd we meet?" she asked.

"I only know this story secondhand. Your mom loves telling us how we met."

"Hi, Chief!" called a voice. Sawyer glanced toward the MacLeods' former front door to find the current owner smiling and waving. Amanda Palermo. He turned to Maddie. "Wait here a minute, will you?"

He jogged over to the woman. "Mind if we pay a visit to your backyard? I was feeling nostalgic and wanted to show Maddie a couple things from the old days. We'll venture down to the creek, too, if you don't mind."

"Go right ahead," Amanda said. "Merry Christmas."

"Merry Christmas," he said.

He headed back to Maddie and took her hand. "Right this way, ma'am."

She slipped her hand into his, and again he loved the way that felt. It had been a while since she'd held his hand before the accident. A while since she'd wanted to be anywhere near him.

"See this spot," he said, pointing beside a bare tree in the backyard not far from the house. "You were making a fort out of a sheet and kiddie chairs, and you had a sandwich and chips on a plate. I came over and told you there was a fat squirrel after your food."

She laughed. "That's how we met?"

"Yup. Then you shouted, 'Let's hide from it!' And you grabbed the plate into the fort and we sat on the grass under the sheet and you offered me half the sandwich and half the chips. We were best friends ever since."

"Aw. Was that the day you and your dad moved next door?"

He nodded. "I went outside and there you were." He couldn't actually remember being five all that well, but her mother had been sitting on the patio and saw and heard the whole thing and loved to tell the story whenever she got nostalgic.

They walked farther down the yard toward the woods. The property extended a half mile, so they'd played in these woods for hours every day as kids. By the creek, he pointed to a flat-topped rock big enough for two butts. "That's where you told me you had a huge crush on Jonathan Walloway in sixth grade. I wasn't interested in girls then, but I remember feeling all out of sorts about the news. By seventh grade, I knew why. You always had boys chasing you, and I was always the BFF."

Maddie looked surprised. "I must have had a big crush on you too."

"Back then you always used to say, 'Nothing is more important to me than our friendship, and therefore nothing can be allowed to ruin it. So even if I want to kiss you, I'm not going to.' And I said, 'So you want to?' And you said, 'It doesn't matter because we can't.' I was so afraid of something ruining us, too, that I never asked if I could kiss you. We just stayed friends. We did go to a couple dances together but just as friends."

"So we dated other people even though we really loved each other?"

"Well, we didn't know we did in middle school and high school," he explained. "I thought you just liked me as a friend, and you thought I just liked you as a friend. It wasn't until prom night that things got very interesting between us."

"Ooh, what happened?"

"I'll have to take you over to the Wedlock Creek Town Hall for that story." He was glad to be leaving the property. He'd left a lot out.

Such as finding his dad passed out drunk on their tiny portion of patio and being unable to wake him up or move him at age nine. Having to ask Ace MacLeod for help so his dad wouldn't freeze to death. Ace not saying a bad word about his dad, just telling Sawyer outright that anytime, day or night, if Sawyer needed help, needed anything, like now, he was to call Ace or April immediately. He'd made Sawyer promise that he'd always reach out to them for help, no matter what. Sawyer had promised. There were so many memories here that he wasn't sure why he'd hit upon that one. Maybe because he'd never forgotten being unable to help his father, passed out in single-degree temps with just a sweatshirt and jeans.

He never wanted to be in a position where he couldn't help, couldn't do anything.

Lots of unknowns where children are concerned, he thought, catching himself by surprise. He'd never thought about that connection. He'd heard people say that having children was like having your heart walk around outside your body. And he certainly couldn't be there to protect his children 24/7. Hell, he'd been standing fifty feet away from where Maddie had crashed her car; he'd *seen* it happen. Unable to stop her, help her.

Maddie took his hand again, shaking him from the memory, from the unsettling direction of his thoughts. In five minutes they were at the hall, where town residents could hold events and where the Wedlock Creek High School prom was held every year.

"We went to the prom together? Just as friends?" she asked as they walked into the hall. It was empty now, light filtering in from the huge oval windows.

"Nope. You went with a date. The guy you liked finally asked you, and you thought it was going to be the start of something. You slow-danced to three songs, and then he talked you into taking a walk to Legend Point."

Maddie narrowed her gaze at him. "Is

this a true story? How do you know how many songs we slow-danced too?"

"Because you told me. Tears streaming down your face."

"Oh. That bad?"

He nodded. "Legend Point is the place where everyone goes to fool around. Or claims to. He got you there and wanted to go further than you were ready for. He got angry and took a wad of dirt and rubbed it on your dress and called you a tease—in a more vulgar way than that—and abandoned you there."

She frowned, wrapping her arms around herself. "Awful."

"Yup. And that's when you called me. To bring you home. But when I found you, sitting with your head down and sobbing between a row of hedges, you couldn't talk or get up, so I just sat and put my arm around your shoulder and you leaned your head against me and cried."

"Poor seventeen-year-old Maddie."

"Yeah. I felt horrible for you. I wanted to kill that jerk. I started telling you how he didn't deserve you, that you were so great, and you said you wished you'd gone to the prom with me, then you popped up and wiped away your tears and said, 'Let's go. We can hang out back and listen to the band and dance if we feel like it.'"

"So in my dirt-smeared dress and... I assume you were in jeans and a T-shirt, we went?"

He nodded. "We stood behind the school, and a slow song came on that you loved, and you put your arms around my neck and your head against my chest and I blurted out, 'Maddie, I love you. I've always loved you.'"

Maddie gasped. "Really? What did I say?"

"You looked up at me with your gorgeous blue eyes and said, 'I've always loved you too.' And then you leaned your head up and kissed me. For the first time on the lips. I almost passed out I was so happy."

She laughed. "Then what happened?"

"We just stayed there and slow-danced through the next five songs. And then I drove us home, and we went down by the creek and sat on that rock and made out and talked about how we'd been so dumb for so many years."

"What about the pact to not ruin the friendship?" she asked.

He smiled just thinking about that moment. "We made a new pact. To never break up."

She threw her arms around him and held on. "I love us. I love Maddie and Sawyer, the seventeen-year-olds."

"Me too. And then suddenly we're talking separation outside a marriage counselor's office with the first snow of the season coming down on our heads." The weight of the world coming down on his, he thought, a jab in his chest.

"I wish we'd been more focused on the first snow, on Christmas, on how much we loved each other."

"You were, until you couldn't take it anymore," he admitted. "You tried—hard."

Snow flurries whipped around them and she looked up. "A sign! A second chance to appreciate what we *do* have."

"That's nice, Maddie, but it's not fair to the woman you were."

"She's not here right now, so it's all I've got," she said with a smile, sticking out her tongue to catch a snowflake.

He laughed, unable to help it. "I don't deserve you, Maddie. How you're able to be so good-humored about any of this is beyond me."

"I probably always was, right? I mean, I *am* me. I'm just not reacting to you based on any kind of history. But the me I am, that has to be the same, right?"

He hadn't really thought about that. But he supposed she was the same old Maddie. Believed in the silver lining. Saw the good. Tried to flip things. She was a nurturer. "Yeah. You're you. The you I fell in love with a long time ago. The you I loved the morning of the accident. The you I love now."

"So no one is separating. No one is getting divorced. We have nephews to take care of."

He was relieved to hear her say that, but again, she wasn't the Maddie who was sick to death of his stalling and "irrational" refusal to take the next step. "What if the twins hadn't been left in our living room in the middle of the night?"

"We'd still have a marriage to save for when I get my memory back," she said, taking his hand. "That's the way I look at

it. And anyway, there are too many vari-
ables for what-ifs."

He held on tight to her bright pink mittened hand, the flurries dancing around
her beautiful face. "With your memory
gone, everything is sunshine and roses
between us. In the back of my mind, I
know that's not fair to you."

"Well, I can't be in a long-term fight
that I don't remember, so I guess we'll
just have to get along."

He smiled. "You will get your memory
back, Maddie."

"I wonder what that will be like. The
old memories mixing with the new."

"Me too," he said, and they started
walking back toward the parking lot,
Maddie keeping her hand on his. He'd
been wondering that a lot. How Maddie
would feel about him.

"Know what else I wonder?" she asked
as she got inside the car.

He got in and they buckled up. "What?"

"How Maddie-with-the-memories will feel when she finds out you're ready to start a family because of the bargain you made with the universe when she was lying unconscious in the hospital."

He stared at her. "She'll be happy. Having a baby is the point. The whole point. It's everything that's standing between us."

"So she'll be happy that you're finally saying yes because she's not dead?" She shook her head. "Okay, it's really weird that I'm talking about myself in the third person, but I'm not the woman you've known since age five. That woman's not back yet. All I know for sure is that it's not how *that* Maddie will want to start a family, Sawyer."

He shook his head, confusion flashing in his green eyes. "What matters is that we'll start a family."

"You love your wife, Sawyer. That's not in question. That's never been in question. But trust me when I say the Maddie I'm coming to know will only want a baby with a man who wants a baby too."

He felt a frown pulling at his face. "The baby should be the point, not the why."

"The why is everything. You think you'll have a baby—the ten babies you promised—and suddenly become all excited about fatherhood? Something that terrifies you and sends you in a dark panic?"

Well, when she put it *that* way.

He got it.

"Let's go pick up the twins," he said, his head starting to pound.

Chapter Seven

A few hours later, Maddie was in the nursery, checking on the sleeping Shane and Max and thinking about the conversation she'd had with Sawyer at the prom site, when her sister popped into mind, Jenna telling her she was pregnant and—

Maddie froze. Jenna was six months along. That was quite obvious; her sister certainly hadn't needed to reveal the news of her pregnancy in the past few days. This recollection was just that—a memory! She could see Jenna's nervous smile. Hear the words *I'm pregnant* com-ing out of her mouth and feel her own combination of pure jealousy and pure joy for her sister.

There was only the snatch of memory. Those few words without context, and she had no sense of where they'd been dur-ing the conversation. But she was sure it was a memory.

She sucked in a deep breath. This was good. This meant her cognitive functions were on the way to returning to normal. She sure hoped she hadn't been as jealous with her sister as she'd felt in that mem-ory; the feeling was unmistakable.

Stephen and I waited. Pregnant to-gether. But—

She could hear those bits of words in Jenna's voice. But that was it.

Still, it was more of the memory.

A headache stirred, and Maddie real-ized she shouldn't push herself too hard to remember. She had to just let it all come in time. As a bit had just now.

Her twin sister had waited? Because of her? That made Maddie feel awful. She could just imagine how gutted she'd been by that realization, how it may have contributed to the strife between her and Sawyer.

Jenna had put off having her first baby out of love and loyalty to Maddie— because Sawyer wasn't ready. And clearly, the writing had been on the wall that Sawyer Wolfe might never be ready. Because Jenna had moved along. Rightfully so.

First a headache, now a stomachache. *Ugh.*

"Everything okay?"

Maddie turned to find Sawyer standing in the doorway. He'd been about make hot chocolate for them when she'd gone up to check on Shane and Max.

"I had a bit of a memory," she said,

hearing the cool bite in her tone. "About my sister, telling me she was pregnant. And a moment later, I remembered just a few words of the conversation. I think my memory is coming back."

He clearly heard the frost in her voice too. He hesitated, then said, "That's great, Maddie."

"Is it?" she whispered. "I mean, of course it is. But look, I'm already mad at you." And none of the good humor and levity of earlier was anywhere in her now.

He shoved his hands into the pockets of his jeans. "Because Jenna and Stephen waited because of me and then felt bad about deciding they couldn't wait anymore. I know. I felt horrible about that. *You* felt horrible about that."

"I'll bet. And if I'm mad at you from just a piece of one memory, imagine how I'll feel when I have them all?"

He gave something of a nod. "Igno-rance isn't really bliss. Maybe for a few days, yes. But it's not reality. I *want* you to have your memory back. That's the real you, Maddie. And the Maddie who knows everything is the Maddie I love. The Maddie I said I'd have ten kids for."

"You say that like it's a plus." Again.

"I say it because, to me, it tells me loud and clear how much I love you, that having you is more important than anything—including my feelings about having children."

"We had this conversation and got nowhere," she said.

Defeat crossed his face. "You know how many times those exact words came out of our mouths over the past year? A million."

"No doubt," she said. When Sawyer had told her they'd been in mediation with a marriage counselor, she hadn't thought much of it. Now she could barely imagine Sawyer talking about his marriage and the problems between them with a therapist. With anyone. They must have hit rock bottom—the sleeping separately, the stony silences. "I'll call Dr. Addison in the morning and let her know about the memory. I started getting a little bit of a headache, so I think it's my brain's way of telling me not to push it."

He nodded. "You'll be back to yourself in no time, Maddie. And that's what we want. Warts and all."

Except he looked a little nervous about that. As nervous as she felt. She liked the way things were, crazy as that sounded. She felt cherished by this man, by her family. She had an immediate purpose in caring for the newborn twins. She felt co-cooned and happy. And as the memories came back, who knew how she'd feel? Angry? Sad? Worried? Unsettled about knowing she'd have her deepest wish fulfilled—to have a baby—only because Sawyer had bargained with the universe and was a man of his word?

Oh yeah, she had a definite feeling Maddie who remembered would not be okay with that.

Sawyer sat at the desk in his home office, Moose lying by his feet, gnawing on a rawhide bone. He'd come in here to check the database connected to the WCPD for the name Russtower, to find out why that surname on his Holiday Happymakers form rang a criminal bell. But he hadn't gotten further than going to the WCPD site. He kept thinking about Maddie and her memory returning.

One small memory had fought its way to the surface of Maddie's mind and the two of them were already in that off-kilter place. Maddie had turned in early, at barely eight thirty, and he wasn't sure if the memory had made her tired or their conversation. Probably both. But her going to bed while he was downstairs felt like old times. In a bad way.

He'd thought telling Maddie about the bargain he'd made when he'd been keeping a bedside vigil would solve the problem. She wanted kids; he'd have ten if only she wasn't taken from him. She'd survived the accident, and now he was making good on his word. But it wasn't enough for Maddie-who-couldn't-remember. According to her, at this point it was less about the agreeing to start a family and more about the wanting to. But wasn't it a compromise? Wasn't that what marriages were based on? Give and take. Finding ways to keep each other happy.

As if he had all the answers. He wasn't getting this right—that was about all he knew for sure.

He heard a cry through the baby monitor next door in the living room and took the stairs two at a time to make sure another shriek didn't wake up Maddie. In the nursery, he found Max waving his arms and scrunching up his face. Saw-

yer reached in and took him out, checking his diaper, which felt reasonably dry,
and then holding the baby against him
while he walked around the room, rubbing the tiny back.

A memory of his own popped into his
mind. An image of Cole trying to make
him a mug of hot tea. Sawyer had been
sick with a bad cold and home alone when
Cole's mother had uncharacteristically
dropped him off at the Wolfe apartment,
angry about something and not checking if their dad was home. Sawyer had
been using scratchy toilet paper for tissues, his nose red and raw, and Cole had
asked if he should go to the drugstore and
get Sawyer tissues and medicine, but the
store was too far for Cole to walk. Cole
had taken it upon himself to make Sawyer tea, and at ten years old had done a
semi-decent job, even if he'd put in way
too much sugar. Apparently that was how
his mother liked her tea.

"Your daddy has a good heart," Sawyer whispered to Max. "Same as I do, even if I don't want kids. No offense," he rushed to say. "If you're staying, I'll take good care of you. I already love you. So no worries, okay? I've got you covered." Saying all that exhausted him, and he sat in the glider chair, staring down at the alert little guy in his arms.

Max stared back.

"You're really quite beautiful," Sawyer whispered. "A perfect little being. You just happen to need everything. Love, nurturing, protection, sustenance, shelter." The blue eyes gazed up at him, full of curiosity. His chest felt tight, and he felt a lump in his throat. "How about a story?" He reached for a board book on the table beside the chair, but given his position and the way the baby was nestled, he couldn't quite reach it. "Made-up one by Uncle Sawyer, then."

Max still stared up at him, and Sawyer

wondered what the baby was thinking. Could babies think? Beyond feeling? He'd have to look that up. Or ask Reed Barelli or Theo Stark, the resident baby experts on the WCPD. Reed had toddler triplets and twin one-year-olds. Theo had quadruplet toddlers. Both men knew more about babies than your average bear.

"Okay, so once upon a time there were two brothers named Sawyer and Cole," he said, then hesitated. Had he meant to say that? Guess so, because it had come out of his mouth. "Where's *this* gonna go?" he asked Max, who was clearly getting so bored by the asides that he was now looking nowhere in particular. "Their dad used to tell Sawyer that Cole probably wasn't even his kid, and that anyone could have green eyes and dark hair," he said. "But Sawyer knew Cole was his brother, just *knew*. Even if they'd looked nothing alike, he'd still know, because that was how it was. You just knew some things."

What the hell was he saying? Was it okay that he was being so honest—out loud? He was aware that you were supposed to talk to babies to boost their brain power and language-processing skills. But it wasn't like Max was actually following what Sawyer was saying, so it seemed okay. He'd text Reed or Theo later and make sure.

"I guess there's some stuff I've always needed to get off my chest," he whispered, and Max looked at him and wrapped his little fist around Sawyer's pinky. Sawyer almost gasped. "I'm surprised you like me, but you seem to. I guess I'm doing all right by you and your brother, though." The baby held on, his grip surprisingly tight.

For a moment, Sawyer just stared at this magical little being, wondering if he might be dreaming this all up. He attempted to pinch his arm with his one free hand, and he felt it, so this must have actually been happening. *I'm talking to a newborn. My nephew. Telling him my life story. His father's life story.* Would wonders ever cease?

"Should I continue the story? Yeah? Okay. So the two brothers, Sawyer and Cole. Cole wanted to be closer to Sawyer, and Cole tried hard to get through for a while, but Sawyer was a stupid preteen and not too interested. Then Sawyer wanted to be closer to Cole, but Cole had no interest. They were never on the same page at the same time. Things get complicated, and people and stupid stuff get in the way."

Such as his dad's girlfriends not wanting another kid around. Cole's mother screaming into the phone at their dad to the point that he'd blocked her calls. And his and Cole's own stupid bravado, not wanting the other to know how much it all hurt. And it had.

He took another long look at the baby

in his arms. Seven pounds, five ounces at birth, according to the paperwork. Twenty-one inches long. Healthy. A tiny marvel. "And then you and *your* brother are born, and it looks like your dad named you guys after Maddie and me. Why, you want to know, since we're not exactly close? Since I was so mad at him for stealing from us that I almost pressed charges against him? But didn't. Maybe that answers the question. Maybe your dad knew I wouldn't, that I might hate him or something close to it since I don't think I could ever hate him, but that I would never truly turn my back on him. He knew he could leave you two here and that we'd take good care of you. And we will, you can count on that. No matter what, you can count on that."

Sawyer stared out the dark window at the slight illumination from the porch light. Flurries were coming down again. The baby in his arms let out a funny sigh, his slate-blue eyes drooping a bit. Max seemed to be fighting it, not wanting to miss anything.

Sawyer smiled. "You'll only be missing my story if you fall asleep, and I'm not sure you want to hear it. Your father and I circling each other for years, never landing."

His smile faded and he looked back out the window, wondering where his brother was, what was going through his mind.

He cradled Max a little tighter against him, his heart ready to burst.

Maddie stood outside the nursery, tears stinging as she accidentally on purpose eavesdropped. She felt only slightly guilty about it. About ten minutes ago, she'd heard one of the babies cry, and by the time she'd fully woken up to get out of bed, she'd heard Sawyer's footsteps coming up the stairs and thought she should let him attend to his nephew. Let him spend a little time alone with a baby.

When he started talking about personal stuff, she thought about tiptoeing back to her room, but she couldn't move. She'd been so touched by what Sawyer was saying. And she had a feeling he hadn't said a quarter as much in marriage counseling as he had in the ten minutes he'd been in the nursery.

"Now, Max," she heard Sawyer continue, "I'll only say this because Shane is fast asleep. You were named after your aunt Maddie, at least we think you were, and that's a pretty big name to live up to. Your aunt Maddie is the best thing that ever happened to me."

Maddie put her hand over her mouth to stifle her gasp. She knew Sawyer loved her, loved his wife, but the reverence in his voice was so touching that her knees almost buckled.

"When you find someone like Maddie,"

he went on, "you give her the world. Everything she wants. Because someone that special deserves everything. I was an idiot for saying no over and over, year after year, to starting a family. I was selfish. Maddie wanted a baby, and I should have said, 'Anything your heart desires.' Because she's that great. And I almost lost her. That's what I meant about agreeing to have ten kids if that's what Maddie wants. Maybe I didn't say it right."

His voice cracked then, and Maddie wrapped her arms around herself and hurriedly tiptoed back to her bedroom. She shouldn't have been listening. He thought she was asleep, not listening to his every word and emotion right outside the nursery.

Sorry, Sawyer, she sent telepathically and got back into bed.

A few moments later, she heard him coming down the hall toward their room. He went downstairs, then came right back up, so he must have just turned off the lights. As she heard him come into the room, she closed her eyes. He kissed the top of her head and then turned around, facing away. Should she leave him with his thoughts? All that heaviosity by himself? If she'd bared her soul to a sleepy baby and *he'd* overheard, she'd want him to hold her, not necessarily to say anything, just to hold her so she wouldn't feel so alone. Yes, as far as she could tell now, she and Sawyer were such different people. She knew that he tended to be a lone wolf, but even a lone wolf needed a pack. She was his pack.

She reached around until she felt his hand, and she held it. He gave it a gentle squeeze but didn't let go.

I love you too, she wanted to say. But she didn't doubt he knew that.

Oh, flip, she thought. *I am who I am, even though I have no memory of myself.* "Sawyer?"

"Yup?"

"I heard everything you said," she blurted out. "I was standing right outside the nursery. I didn't mean to eavesdrop, but then I couldn't stop listening."

He was silent for a moment. Then another. Then he turned around to face her in the dim lighting of the moon. "Who needs a therapist when there are newborns to talk to at all hours?"

She gave him a gentle smile. "I like what you said about me."

"All true," he said, reaching out to touch her face. "Every word."

"I understand a bit better about the ten babies. The bargain and what it meant to you to make it. I might not completely agree, but I understand more now."

"Good," he said. "Because I couldn't explain it well for some reason. Only to a droopy-eyed infant."

She squeezed his hand. "I've been so focused on my memory and the babies and us that I haven't really stopped to think about your relationship with Cole and how all this is affecting you. You really love him, don't you?"

"Of course I do. He's disappointed me a bunch of times, but he's the kid I wanted to protect for so many years that it's ingrained. I always felt so powerless when it came to Cole and my family." He narrowed his eyes as if he'd just realized that this moment. "I still do," he whispered. "He's been headed down the wrong path, and he's either gonna keep going or turn around. I want him to turn around."

"I hope he does."

"Me too."

"I'm going to finish up a little more paperwork," he said, slipping out of bed. "I'll be up in about an hour."

"Okay," she said. She didn't want him to go. But she knew he needed to be alone with his thoughts and the knowledge that she'd heard everything he'd said. She'd been hoping he'd wrap his arms around her and they'd just fall asleep, no need to talk more, but maybe the intimacy was a little too much for him.

One day at a time. Just like Dr. Addison had told her in the hospital when she'd come to. *Don't try to rush it*, the doctor had said. And that went for husbands too.

Chapter Eight

Maddie hadn't gotten much sleep. Sawyer hadn't come up to bed until well after midnight, and she'd been so tired she'd fallen right back to sleep. But before then, she'd tossed and turned, thinking about everything they'd talked about. What she'd overheard. And the memory she'd had of her and her sister talking about Jenna's pregnancy.

She figured it would be helpful to know if she was remembering accurately. In the middle of the night it had occurred to her that she might have imagined the whole thing based on what she'd been told. She doubted that but wanted to check anyway. Plus, maybe talking about the memory would open it up a little inside her head, allow her to remember more.

So after making sure that Sawyer was okay with being on his own with the twins, Maddie texted Jenna to ask her to breakfast, adding that she remembered something and wanted to talk it over. Jenna had texted back an immediate Ooh! Dee's Diner at 8 sharp. Maddie had headed out through the front door just in time to hear one twin crying in the nursery.

"I could just go see—" she said, coming back inside and taking off her gloves.

"Nope." Sawyer gently turned her around. "I've got this. I need to learn how to take care of them the same as you do. We're an equal opportunity aunt and uncle."

And lucky for him, the crying stopped.

"Ah, see, your mom told me the other day not to rush in at first cry," he said, "but to wait a good ten seconds and they might soothe themselves back to sleep. So go before they both wake up and start bawling. Besides, you need to talk to Jenna. Oh—and you love the blueberry pancakes at Dee's. With bacon."

"Does anyone not love that?"

"I actually don't like blueberry pancakes. I'm an omelet guy. With the bacon and cheddar inside. And a big order of hash browns."

"Did we used to go there for breakfast a lot?"

He nodded. "Lunch too. You love their grilled cheese. With bacon."

"We'll have to go sometime," she said.

The crying started up again. He smiled and kissed her on the cheek. "See you later. Take your time. I'm only expected at the precinct part-time this week, so don't rush back on my account."

I'd rush back because I want to be with you. And the twins.

It was cold but not killer cold, so she put her gloves back on and walked the five minutes to Dee's, which was just a few doors down from MacLeod's Multiples Emporium. She found Jenna waiting at a booth in the back by the window.

Jenna started to slide out, then said, "Oh, who am I kidding?" and slid back in. "I wanted to give you a hug, but my days of getting up and down easily are over."

Maddie laughed. "Hug accepted in spirit from across the table."

"How are you feeling?" Jenna asked, handing Maddie a menu.

"Pretty good. My goose egg is almost gone, and with a little concealer, the scratch is barely noticeable. How are *you* feeling?"

"Not bad. I can't sleep on my stomach anymore or my right side, but Stephen got me this great body pillow, and it's helping me get comfortable."

"I can't wait to meet my new niece and nephew," Maddie said with a smile.

"I love that my twins will have instant cousins. Or cousins-ish."

Maddie laughed. "So let's order, and then I'll tell you about the memory I mentioned."

"I'm so glad to hear you remembered something!" Jenna said. "I hope you don't mind, but I let Mom and Dad know. They're so hopeful for what this means. That you're on the mend."

"I spoke to my doctor this morning, and she said it's a great sign." Dr. Addison had been elated to hear the news but did caution Maddie from trying to think too hard, to remember too much. Maddie was supposed to let the memories come naturally, the way the one had last night.

They spent the next couple of minutes figuring out what they wanted. Maddie wasn't in the mood for blueberry pancakes. But Sawyer's omelet sure sounded good. She ordered that, and Jenna went for what she was craving: French toast drizzled in maple syrup.

Once they had their decaf coffees, Maddie told Jenna about the memory, the snippet of conversation. "So does that sound right? Did I remember an actual conversation?"

Jenna's expression had turned a little… uneasy. "Yes. It was right after I found out I was pregnant. I told you the minute the plus sign appeared on the stick. There was no way I could keep the news from you, Maddie."

"I feel awful that you and Stephen felt like you had to wait until Sawyer came around to start a family. That's not right. Not in the slightest."

Jenna reached out a hand and squeezed

Maddie's. "It wasn't really like that. We'd always talked about being pregnant with our first babies at the same time. A twin-palooza. And I wasn't really ready until I hit thirty. I admit that I did start to feel a little antsy the past couple of years. But how could I go ahead without you—especially when Sawyer wasn't budging on the subject?"

"Oh, Jenna. What a cruddy position to be in. I am so sorry."

"It's complicated, Maddie. But Stephen said enough was enough, and so I let you know I was tossing my birth controls in the trash."

"You did? How'd that conversation go?"

"I couldn't not tell you. I tell you everything, Mads. Same for you. We've always been very close."

Maddie felt tears well up and her throat go tight. She barely knew this person sitting across from her, her own twin sister, and she loved her so much at this moment it was as if she hadn't lost all memory of her. "Please tell me I was thrilled for you and excited and didn't burst into tears."

"You were honest. You told me you were very happy for me and hoped I'd get pregnant that night. And then you told me you were jealous as hell and wished your stubborn husband would magically change his mind. Want to know what else you said?"

Maddie grimaced. "Is it bad?"

Jenna laughed. "It's kind of funny. You said maybe he'd get conked on the head by a perp and suddenly want kids."

"Oh my God, I said that?"

"Yup."

"But instead it was me who got conked on the head. And forgot all about wanting a baby so badly I made my own sister feel bad about being pregnant."

"You never made me feel bad, Maddie. I felt bad because of the situation."

The waitress appeared with steaming plates that smelled and looked delicious.

Maddie cut a piece of her bacon and cheese omelet. "Ah, this is good. No wonder it's Sawyer's favorite here."

"I did notice you ordered his favorite. Interesting. Like you want to be closer to him."

Maddie raised an "oh, please" eyebrow. "By eating his favorite breakfast?"

"When you and I went to Cheyenne for a baby expo for a few days, I ate a lot of Stephen's favorites for that very reason. I missed him."

"I'll bet I didn't order any of Sawyer's favorites," Maddie said.

"Oh, you sure did. You love that man. Tough situation and all."

Maddie pushed around her home fries, thinking of Sawyer at home with the twins. "He's taking care of Shane and Max on his own this morning. Talk about complicated." She thought about all she'd heard last night, and her heart ached for Sawyer.

"Right? Between caring for babies and the fact that they're his brother's… No word from Cole?"

Maddie took a sip of her coffee. "Nope. Sawyer's texted him every day to let him know the babies are fine. I wonder if that will keep him away or make him want to come back."

"What do you mean?"

"If the babies are fine, then Cole may feel they're in better hands and stay away. Or being reminded of his children, that they're fine and not with him, may make him feel unsettled and itchy for them. He could have signed away his parental rights at the hospital. He didn't."

"Do you think he'll come back?" Jenna asked, forking a big piece of French toast and swiping it in syrup.

"I really don't know. If I could remember him, maybe I'd have more of a clue."

"How's Sawyer doing with the babies? Does he hate taking care of them? He seemed fine with them the other day."

"He doesn't seem to hate it at all. I can tell it's weird for him, to have them in the house. But some of that has to do with his brother, I think. All it's engendering for him. He's good at babysitting. He's so sweet with them."

"Maybe this is exactly what Sawyer needed. A chance to see firsthand what it's like to have babies in the house, to care for them."

"I was thinking that too. My only worry is that there's a brick wall in that chest of his."

"Blocked, huh?"

Maddie nodded. "It's been building since he was a little kid."

"Well, between you and those adorable twins, that wall just might be blasted through." Jenna finished her decaf and insisted on paying for breakfast. She had to get to MacLeod's since a new salesperson was starting today. The Christmas season apparently had the shop packed every day. Maddie was looking forward to getting back to work soon. But she'd be little help managing the store without any knowledge of the place.

After she walked Jenna to the shop and gave her sister a big hug, she headed home, thinking about what Jenna said. About how the wall could be blasted through.

Maddie thought it was a real possibility. Based on the Sawyer she knew now, she saw glimpses of someone struggling to change. Maybe that was more wishful thinking.

What really had her off balance was the realization that when she got her memory back, everything was going to be different.

* * *

In the hour Maddie had been gone, he'd had three calls from the MacLeods. Two from April, and one from Ace. April was checking to make sure he didn't need any help; she'd be happy to come over. Ace had called to say there was no shame in asking for help and that he was all thumbs when he had newborn twins.

I don't have newborn twins. They're not mine, he'd wanted to say.

But were they? Was their father ever coming back?

Sawyer couldn't answer that. So he'd turned down the offers of assistance this morning and said he was doing just fine on his own.

He hadn't been doing all that great, actually. Shane had screamed bloody murder for fifteen minutes before Sawyer had been able to calm him down. Turned out he'd needed to burp and had diaper rash. A good pat on the tiny back and some ointment and cornstarch, and Fussy-pants was good as new. Then his brother started in. No need to burp. No diaper rash. Not wet. Sawyer had finally struck gold when he held cradled Max in his arms and rocked him from side to side while singing a Beatles song. Max clearly liked the Beatles.

Last night, when he'd held Max in the nursery, taking care of a baby seemed so easy. *Sure*, he'd said to Maddie. *Go, no rush, take your time. I've got this.* Ha. He'd been so smug.

I heard everything you said...

He liked how honest she was. Maddie-with-her-memory would have probably come clean, too, but the past few weeks had been so strained that maybe she wouldn't have. It all might have seemed too much.

But once again, he was in his house, a baby in his arms, unsure if this was forever or not. If this was the new normal.

Good thing he'd attended one of Reed Barelli's classes on caring for multiples ages-zero-to-three-months at the community center, because he'd learned—

Wait a minute. Yes. That was it. That was where he'd heard the name Russ-tower—the surname on the second Holiday Happymakers envelope. A couple months ago, Reed, one of his detectives, had called in a break-in at the community center where he taught his multiples class early in the morning before the traditional workday to make it easier for fathers to attend, since they could bring their babies. Overnight, someone had stolen the props the teachers used for the various baby classes—bottles, burp cloths, diapers, even the curved pad for baby changing. Sawyer had been a couple of doors down and had come over to help with the investigation. He'd asked Maddie if MacLeod's could let the center borrow some items until they were replaced, and of course the MacLeods donated a heap of new baby paraphernalia—all within fifteen minutes so that Reed's class could go on as planned.

Sawyer had stuck around the class, going over the list of registrants, which had included a petty thief named Vince Russtower. Russtower had shown up for class with a one-month-old baby and was struggling; Reed had spent a lot of time with him, repositioning his baby son in his arms, helping him angle the bottle. Reed was sure a few items in Russtower's bag looked like a few of the stolen items, including a blue-and-white baby blanket, but he couldn't be sure, and the case had gone cold.

Sawyer put Shane back in his carrier beside his brother, picked both up and went inside his office. He settled them on the floor, both babies looking at the pastel spinning mobiles attached to the carriers. They seemed happy enough for now.

He reached into the basket on his desk for the envelope from Holiday Happymakers. The one from Jake Russtower. He typed Russtower into the database. Bingo. Vince Russtower had been arrested twice this year for petty theft. He'd stolen a package of steak from the grocery store, and the manager and owner had decided to drop the charges. Then he'd stolen a chocolate heart from the Valentine's Day aisle at the drugstore, and the manager had also declined to follow through with charges, so the case had been dropped. Sawyer had no doubt Vince had been the one to steal the baby items from the community center; it was the guy's MO. A sad MO, at that. A package of steak. A chocolate heart for his wife. Baby bottles and a baby blanket. It was theft all the same, but the kind of theft that made Sawyer think about a person's bank account and desperation.

Sawyer pulled Jake's request out of the envelope and read it again.

I'm not getting anything for Christmas because my father only cares about his stupid new wife and always-crying new baby. I could use a bike so I don't have to ask him for rides anywhere. Whatever. This is just fake Santa. I'm sure I won't be getting anything.
—Jake Russtower.

Something in the kid's tone had gotten under his skin, reminded him of himself at that age, he guessed. Sawyer usually volunteered at the community center once a month and knew they had a kids' group there that met after school and on weekends. And now there was a new baby at home—and the new wife. He'd stop by the center tomorrow and see if Jake hung out there. There was strong outreach in the schools to make sure kids who seemed troubled or distracted were aware of the center, so there was a good chance Jake did go there. He'd check on him, make sure the kid was okay.

He heard a key in the front door, and he took the carriers over to say hi to Maddie.

"The bits of conversation I recalled with Jenna really happened," she said, taking off her gloves and hat and putting them in a basket by the door. "My memory is definitely on its way back."

That had never been in any doubt, but he was glad she'd gotten that confirmed for herself.

"I had your favorite at Dee's. Mmm, those home fries were amazing."

He smiled. "I wouldn't mind having some right now."

"Then it's a good thing I got you a bacon and cheese omelet with a side of home fries to go," she said, holding up a white bag.

He was starving and grateful. "That was very thoughtful. Thank you."

"Kiddos give you any trouble?"

"Well, they did scream their heads off for longer than usual, but I managed to get it under control. Look at them now—so curious and alert. You'd never know they'd almost punctured my eardrums a half hour ago."

Maddie laughed. "Well, how about I take these guys into the living room for story time while you eat your breakfast."

He was about to tell her he'd prefer they all joined him in the kitchen, but she'd already picked up the carriers and headed to the living room. Which was interesting because, for a while there, he'd been counting the minutes until she got back so he wasn't solely responsible for the twins. Sometimes they were easy; sometimes they were a heck of a lot of work, and four hands were better than two with two tiny rabble-rousers.

As he went into the kitchen with his takeout and sat down to eat alone, he had to admit he missed Maddie and the babies. He poured himself a mug of coffee, struck by the notion that needing help with them and missing them were two very different things.

Talk about getting under his skin. The newborns had burrowed under the way Maddie had when he was too young to know to keep her out. He'd actually once told the marriage counselor exactly that when she'd asked how he'd managed to get himself married when he'd vowed never to have a family. A wife was family, the counselor had pointed out. Unnecessarily, he might have added.

Because Maddie has always been family, he'd explained. He'd loved her from his earliest memories. The counselor had tried to open up his mind to what that meant, but Sawyer hadn't been having it. Then she'd tried to connect it to his push-pull with his brother, whom he'd also loved from his earliest memories, even if the relationship had rarely been easy, and he hadn't been having that either. Twice, he'd walked out of the room. Maddie had been pissed as hell both times.

So what does it all mean? he asked himself the way the counselor might have. The problem was that Sawyer didn't want to know, didn't want to think about it. That was Maddie's true issue with him. The refusal to dig deep, to "do the work," as she called it. At the time he'd thought, *Lord, save me from Dr. Phil.* But now all he could think was that if he'd "done the work," if he'd dug, Maddie would never have gotten into that car accident. She wouldn't have lost her memory.

He sighed and sat down, his appetite gone, but he opened up the container and ate, since Maddie had been nice enough to bring it home for him. He popped a home fry into his mouth, listening to Maddie tell the boys a story about a striped purple rabbit named Bunnito with long, floppy green ears. Her story was so ridiculous that he found himself smiling, everything forgotten but her melodic voice and the silly antics of Bunnito. He ate his breakfast, enjoying every bite now, finishing up so that he could join them in the living room.

He *wanted* to be with them. His wife and the newborns. He did miss them. Well, they *were* his abandoned nephews—of course they'd gotten under his skin. Of course he wanted to take care of them along with the wife he loved.

He wondered if that bit of introspection counted as "doing the work." He could hear Maddie in his mind saying: *Are you freaking kidding me? You're rationalizing. Abandoned—please. You love them. Just admit it—to yourself if not to me.*

Same as you'd love your own babies if you'd let yourself have them.

Wow, did he know his wife well. Himself, not so much.

Sawyer had to go into the PD for several hours that afternoon to guide his rookie through a difficult case, and good old-fashioned police work had taken his mind off home. The precinct, the protocol, his staff—all of it so familiar that he'd relaxed the moment he'd arrived, unaware of how tight his shoulders had been until the muscles actually unbunched and knots came loose.

That he was better as a cop than he'd ever be as a father was not news.

"You're like the dad I never had," Justin Mobley said then, making Sawyer do a double take. Sawyer had been explaining a tricky issue regarding search and seizure when Mobley clapped him on the shoulder and made the pronouncement.

"What?" Sawyer managed on a cough.

"I was raised by a single mom who was great, but whenever I'm mentored by an older gentleman, I feel like I have a dad in those moments."

"Mobley, I appreciate the sentiment, but I'm *thirty-two*. Not fifty-two."

Mobley tilted his head and examined Sawyer's face. "Are you? You seem older. You don't *look* older. You just *seem* older."

"That's because I'm the chief, Mobley. Wise beyond my years. Experience will do that to you."

"What's Barelli's excuse?" Officer Benitez joked, tossing a wad of paper at Reed.

"Hilarious," Reed said, tossing it back.

Ah, Sawyer could stay here all day. And night. Sometimes he had, when the thought of going home had seemed…like an argument waiting for him. That had been wrong. He realized that now. He needed to be more like Maddie—to face things head-on, to blurt out the truth, to ask the questions. Not take cover like a perp. Hide. Hope not to get caught.

That wasn't who he wanted to be.

"Hey, Reed," he said, turning in his swivel chair toward the detective. "Do newborns think? Or do they just feel? It's not like they can follow a conversation."

Reed raised an eyebrow. "They know if they want something, even if they're not sure what that is—food, a dry diaper, a cuddle, a burp, a bottle."

"But if I'm, say, thinking out loud to Max and Shane, I won't be scarring them for life?"

Reed smiled. "Not until they're at least eighteen months."

"Good to know, thanks, Barelli." He swiveled back around, wondering if eighteen months from now the twins would still be in the nursery, Cole nowhere to be found.

He had to get his mind off his brother.

He wrapped up the day at the police station, then stopped by the community center to see if Jake Russtower was part of the after-school group. He realized he had no idea what the kid looked like. *Good police work, there, Wolfe.* But then he saw Vince Russtower come through the door, wave at a kid, who jogged over, and Vince put the kid's backpack over his own shoulder and they walked out, chatting. Huh. Not the family scene Sawyer had envisioned based on Jake's anger-tinged Holiday Happymakers form, but looks could be deceiving. So could requests for bikes.

He couldn't get a handle on it, so he figured he'd do a little sussing out of the situation. He told the director he was thinking about volunteering with the kids' group for an hour after work, and the guy was thrilled and said they could use all the support they could get. Sawyer said he'd start tomorrow.

By the time he got home, it was past six. Maddie had let Moose out in the yard, but he owed the German shepherd a walk. Moose didn't love the cold in his older age, but he did like walking on powdery snow, and last night had left a fine couple of inches on the ground. Forty-five minutes later, they returned home. Maddie was in the kitchen, saying she was heating up the last of the lasagna, if that sounded good to him. Lasagna always sounded good.

Dinner was weird. *He* was being weird. And Maddie was reacting to it, tiptoeing around it at first and then doing what she did best: facing the issue head-on.

"You're being weird. Why? Because of last night?"

He almost choked on his bite of gooey, delicious lasagna. "Last night?"

"You know I overheard you say some pretty personal things, Sawyer. Things

I didn't know because I don't remember anything."

He put his fork down. "Yeah, I guess. I've been doing a lot of thinking these past several days. Or trying to. I get to one conclusion and then, whammo, something else seems right. Or wrong."

"Yeah, I know what you mean. Well, let's just eat, then, and keep it light. We could both use a break from the big stuff."

He covered her hand with his in appreciation, then they ate and talked about funny things the twins and Moose had done that day. Sawyer insisted on kitchen cleanup and Maddie said she'd luxuriate in a long, hot bubble bath. Which had him thinking about her in the bath. Naked. Some nights over the past year, the heightened emotions between them still led to sex. Other nights, those emotions led to the couch. Alone. He missed sex with Maddie. So much he couldn't take it sometimes.

Once the babies were fed and changed and played with and read to and finally asleep in the nursery, they decided to watch a goofy buddy comedy. Sawyer made popcorn, and they sat on the sofa and watched the movie, Sawyer laughing so hard at a few points that Moose came over to check on him. The comedy had been what they'd both needed. Their moods lightened, they headed upstairs, mimicking lines from the movie, and Maddie was fast asleep by the time he came out of the bathroom. He stood there watching her sleep for a minute, then got in beside her, facing her back, and dared put his arm around her. She stirred but didn't wake up, and he relaxed.

The next thing he knew, Moose was letting out a low growl. Alerting. The room was dark now, moonlight spilling in through the curtains. Sawyer had clearly fallen asleep. He bolted up, grabbing his service weapon from the bedside table.

Then he heard the noise. Someone was on the porch. At—he looked at his phone—2:18 a.m. Gun in hand, he got out of bed and hurried downstairs, moving to the side of the door and ready to announce himself as a police officer to whoever was out there.

He heard a movement. Then footsteps—leaving. At something of a distance, a car peeling out.

Holy hell, he knew *that* sound.

Cole Wolfe's beater car.

Sawyer threw open the door just in time to see the red taillights whip around Main Street. A small shopping bag, with a logo from a baby emporium in nearby Brewer, was on the porch. He took it inside, putting the gun away in the safe in the hallway closet.

So what is this? he wondered, opening the bag. Inside were two baby-sized cowboy hats, yellow straw with brown leather trim.

You and me will be cowboys one day, galloping after outlaws! Cole used to say all the time when he was young, seven, eight, nine, pretending both hands were rifles and making *ka-pow* noises while running in circles. Sawyer had always told him that cowboys rode after cattle, not outlaws; that was what cops did, and Sawyer was planning on becoming a cop. Cole said not him, he was going to be an outlaw-chasing cowboy.

Except now Cole likely felt like the outlaw.

Sawyer looked at the tiny cowboy hats, his heart heavier than he could handle. He shoved the hats back into the bag and went inside, goose bumps on his arms from the cold. And the surprise. The shock.

"What's that?"

Sawyer glanced up to find Maddie coming down the stairs, tying the sash of her robe around her waist.

"Cole." He explained about the noise. And handed her the bag.

She looked inside and gasped. "Do you know what I just heard in my head? Cole saying he was going to be a cowboy one day. Is that a memory?"

Sawyer nodded. "I was just thinking about that myself. I'm just not sure what he's trying to say with this."

She pulled out a mini cowboy hat and turned it in her hand, then glanced at the logo on the shopping bag. "Well, he avoided MacLeod's and went to Brewer to find these."

"He avoided us too. He could have rung the bell and come in. Instead, he chose to drop these off at two in the morning, then rush away. And not just some random gifts. Cowboy hats. That means something to him."

"Is he saying goodbye?" Maddie asked, and he saw tears shining in her eyes.

Hell, now he felt tears stinging his own eyes. He shrugged, unable to speak.

Maddie put down the bag and came over and wrapped her arms around him, and he held her tight, burying his face against the side of her neck.

Don't let go, don't let go, he silently whispered. To her.

She didn't let go. They stood there in the dark hallway, Moose now lying down by the door, his chin on his paw.

"Sawyer," she whispered, "are you worried he's not coming back or that he is coming back?"

"I don't know. That's what has me so off-kilter. Of course I want him to come back. He's their father. You think I want them to grow up knowing their father left him with us and took off, but oh, he did buy you guys little cowboy hats." He let out a harsh laugh and shook his head. "My father was a crappy dad, but he was there. He didn't take off on me." He froze for a second as a sensation like sludge or quicksand flung itself around inside his chest.

My father never took off on me. He was always there. Not literally every day or night. But never gone for more than a couple of days. I don't recall ever worrying he'd just disappear on me.

Because I knew he loved me deep down? That he did care?

Maybe.

He thought about Vince Russtower picking up Jake from the community center. Carrying his son's backpack as they left. There might have been some tension in the home, but what he saw—and granted, it was only once—it said a lot. Russtower was *there*. That Holiday Happymakers form had lodged in his stomach with the force of a heavyweight's fist, and it eased up some now that he thought about it in this new light.

"Let's go to bed, Sawyer." She took his

hand and led him upstairs, and he silently followed her.

She got into bed and so did he, and when she turned onto her side to face him, he did the same. She reached out a hand to touch his face and then kissed him. Gently at first and then not so gently. And then she took off his T-shirt and ran her hands all over his chest, kissing his neck and his pecs, the cool, soft hands everywhere.

By the time she got to his sweats, he was beyond thought and only *felt*.

Chapter Nine

A crying baby woke Maddie at four forty-five, which was almost a reasonable time to wake up. Sawyer was fast asleep beside her, and for a moment she just watched him sleep, marveling at how good-looking he was. The straight, strong profile. The thick dark hair. The five-o'clock shadow.

She wondered if she was a control taker in bed all the time or if she'd simply done what the moment had called for last night. And what an amazing moment it was.

Sawyer had responded instantly, and the experience had been so emotional, so intimate, that Maddie had almost cried a time or two until ecstasy had won out. Sex with Sawyer was everything she'd imagined it would be the past several days. She was glad they hadn't waited for her memory to return. She had two tiny memories back now, which meant more would be coming each day. She'd wanted to be with Sawyer as the woman she was now, the one who was getting this rare chance to fall in love with him all over again.

Falling in love without all the history, though, she reminded herself. That wasn't falling in love. That was fantasy.

She frowned, wishing she could stop thinking for just a minute, but *without* a history to call from, her mind wasn't exactly full. She had a lot of space to fill.

The cry came harder, so Maddie reluctantly got out of bed and headed into the nursery.

"What's the matter, little guy?" she said, picking up Shane, whose shrieks instantly stopped as she cradled him against her and rubbed his back. "Let's get you changed."

Once both infants had fresh diapers and pajamas, she brought them downstairs in their carriers to feed them in the living room. She had Shane in her arms when Sawyer came down the stairs, all rumpled and sexy. She blushed thinking about last night, which made her feel silly until she realized it was the first time for her.

"I'll admit I was hoping to wake up next to you and have a repeat of last night," he said.

She grinned. "Me too. But duty called."

"I know I said I didn't think we should be intimate until your memory came back, but to be honest, I've felt so close to you, Maddie. Everything about last night felt so natural."

"I know exactly what you mean," she said, her heart doing somersaults.

A shrill cry came from Max. Translation: *Uh, what about my bottle?*

She smiled. "I made a bottle for Max, too—it's in the kitchen."

He went to get it, then came back, scooped up Max and sat down beside her. She watched him coo at the baby, angling the bottle just so. What was also natural? The way Sawyer was with his nephews.

When Max finished his bottle, Sawyer held him upright and patted his back, then repositioned him in his arms to let him stare out the big sliding glass doors to the deck, the snow still slightly clinging to the trees. "I'm going to look for Cole today," he said.

Maddie stared at him. "Really?"

"I have to talk to him. I imagine him out there, tortured and going crazy, unable to live with himself for dropping off his babies and leaving, but unable to keep them either. That he came to the house to leave gifts tells me he cares—a lot."

Maddie nodded. "It's clear that he cares. I want to come with you to look for him. I'll ask my parents to watch the twins for the day. It's probably better that you talk to him without Shane and Max right there. That might be too much for Cole."

"Agreed. And I'm glad you want to come, Maddie. You might not remember Cole yet, but he always liked you, and having you there will likely relax him. If we even find him."

"Have any ideas about where to look?"

"A few," Sawyer said. "I did a search online a couple days ago actually, but he moved out of the most recent address last Monday—just a few days before he showed up here with the twins."

"Was he evicted? That might help explain him feeling so desperate—alone with newborns, nowhere to live?"

"I spoke to his landlord. Cole hadn't paid rent in two months. He supposedly worked at the rodeo on the outskirts of town, mucking out stalls, that kind of thing, but he was let go. I haven't been able to find a trace of him since, not with a place of employment or home address."

"I hope we find him."

"Me too," Sawyer said, eyeing the bag with the baby cowboy hats on the coffee table.

After two cups of coffee each and eggs and toast, Maddie called her mom, who was excited about babysitting the twins for the day. They were the new store mascots. Within an hour, Maddie and Sawyer had dropped them off, stopped back at the house to take Moose on a walk and were ready to start the search.

"So where to?" Maddie asked as she buckled up. "Think he's still in town?"

"I'm not sure. I didn't even know where he lived. Isn't that crazy?"

"It happens. Families pull apart, relatives get estranged. It's not crazy, just sad that it happens."

"I wish all families could be like yours," he said. "That was the only thing I was ever really envious of as a kid. That my family—if you could call it that—wasn't like yours."

"Of course your family was a family. Even just you and your dad and Cole from afar. That's a family."

"I guess," he said. He started the car and didn't respond, and Maddie got the feeling he needed a break from the conversation. Seemed to her, though, that it was exactly the conversation Sawyer needed to have. Family meant something sad and scary to him, something he couldn't count on. Seven years of marriage hadn't changed that for him. A solid, happy marriage—

until this past year when her biological clock began ticking away.

She was pretty sure that was what had her—the Maddie she'd been—so upset. That their beautiful union hadn't changed his notion of what a family was.

Sawyer pulled onto the freeway, taking the exit for Brewer, which was a half hour from Wedlock Creek. "I'm going to start with the hospital where the twins were born. He might have left his new address when he filled out forms. *If* he filled out forms. Worth a try. He has to be living *somewhere*."

"Sawyer. I just realized something. We were likely in that hospital when Gigi gave birth. When Cole was there, pacing in front of the nursery—you were sitting by my bedside in the hospital, waiting for me to wake up from the car accident. I didn't even think of that till just now."

He almost stopped short. "You're right. That's nuts."

Brewer County Hospital was in a stately old brick building. Maddie recalled leaving there the other day, although she had no memories about being there before.

They followed signs for Labor and Delivery, which was on the fourth floor.

"We were both born here," Sawyer said in the elevator. Four months, three days apart. "I'm the older one."

She smiled. "Was Cole born here too?"

"Yup. And now his children."

And maybe our children. If we have any. She was very sure they would. And not because Sawyer had made a bargain with God or the universe or whomever he'd been praying to when he'd kept his bedside vigil. They'd have a baby because he wanted to have a baby just as she did. Not for any other reason.

She, Maddie-without-her-memory, believed that. Just as Maddie-with-her-memory believed all these years.

Why she had faith in that, in him, she

really wasn't sure. The past seven years should have been telling her otherwise. But the man she'd come to know, this Sawyer since she'd come to in this very hospital, the Sawyer who was caring for his newborn nephews, was not the man he'd been before the accident, before the twins arrived. *That* she believed.

As they approached the nurses' station, a nurse came over and gave Maddie a hug. "Hi! Great to see you. Volunteering this week?"

Maddie had volunteered here? She glanced at Sawyer, but he gave her something of a shrug. "I'm recuperating from a car accident so not totally on the mend yet, but give me a couple weeks and I'm sure I'll be back."

"Good, because you're wonderful with the NICU babies." The woman smiled and headed toward a patient's room.

"I volunteered here?" she whispered to

Sawyer. "In the neonatal intensive care unit? You didn't mention that."

"I had no idea. But I'm not surprised. You love babies and you love to help. I do wonder why you didn't tell me." He looked toward the nursery window, where they could just see bassinets and a nurse holding a baby. "Actually, I guess I know why you didn't tell me."

Maddie did too. Volunteering in the NICU must have felt like something she didn't want to share with Sawyer—the man who was denying her a baby. She could see herself not thinking that Sawyer would get it or understand—including how bittersweet it must have been for her to be around the newborns.

He dropped down onto a bench, and Maddie sat beside him. "I really pushed you away, didn't I? I know you have no recollection of any of this. But I do. And I'm sorry." He shook his head, seeming pretty disappointed in himself.

She put a hand on his shoulder. "Hey. Let's go ask about Cole," she said gently.

He nodded, and they stood and headed back over to the nurses' station. "I'm Sawyer Wolfe, the chief of police in Wedlock Creek," he said, holding up his identification. "This isn't a police matter, but I just wanted you to know I'm a solid citizen. My brother, Cole Wolfe, is the father of male twins born here last Thursday. We're caring for the twins for a while, but I'm wondering if Cole left behind an address."

The nurse eyed him and his ID again, then clicked some keys on her computer. "I couldn't give you his information even if it were here, but I can tell you it's not. Only the mother's address appears on the intake forms. I don't see any information for the father, Cole Wolfe. But I do see him listed as the father and that he left with the discharged babies last Thursday."

So much for that. Sawyer thanked her,

and they left the hospital, both of them quiet on the way to the car. They buckled up in silence, and Maddie's gaze was drawn out the window while Sawyer drove back toward Wedlock Creek. He must have had a destination in mind.

A glance out the window told her they were on the outskirts of town, heading toward the river, where she and Sawyer used to sneak into one of the abandoned, dilapidated old cabins after school and talk about life—

She went stock-still. Another memory. This one was so vivid, so full. Her and Sawyer as teenagers, sharing the pistachio nuts she was addicted to in those days, sitting cross-legged beside each other, telling secrets. She'd share her crushes, trying to make hers on Sawyer go away. He never talked about his crushes, and she'd thought then that he was private about that stuff. She'd never had a clue he was as in love with her as she'd been with him. She waited for more of the memory, more knowledge of them, to come, but it all faded away.

"Maddie? What's wrong? You truly look like you saw ghost."

"Another memory," she said. "I remember the cabin. Going there to share our secrets."

He gave her a warm smile. "I'm glad you're remembering, Maddie. And so far all good times."

"That's a lucky break," she said. "For both of us. We kept the biggest secret of all from each other at that cabin, though. That we loved each other."

"Yup. I was bursting with it, but I couldn't tell you."

"What's the connection to Cole at the cabins?"

"He's the one who told me about the place. For three or four years when we were kids, the cabins were a mess. The owner abandoned the property, but there were legalities involved, so the bank couldn't foreclose for a long time. I stopped going once the place was sold, but Cole told me he used to sneak there all the time in the off-season. He found comfort in the place and loved the river. I could see him renting a cabin for cheap in the weeks before Christmas when business is slow."

As Sawyer turned onto a dirt road, Maddie saw the sign for RiverView Cabins, 1.5 miles. A clearing came into view, and Maddie could see identical log structures a good distance apart, facing the river. He pulled up in front of the first cabin with a big Rental Office sign on it.

A woman wearing a hunter-green sweatshirt with a RiverView Cabins logo and a name pin that read Joanna Miles stood and smiled at them. "Welcome! Interested in renting a cabin?"

"Actually, we're hoping if you can tell us if Cole Wolfe is staying here. I'm his brother, Chief Sawyer Wolfe of the Wedlock Creek PD."

"I thought you looked familiar," Joanna said. "He was here, the past two nights, actually, but he checked out bright and early, just before eight a.m."

Maddie glanced at the clock on the wall. It was barely eight thirty. They'd just missed him. "Did he, by any chance, mention where he was headed?"

"Only thing he said was that he was starting his new job this morning, and it came with room and board. Nice guy— he left a ten-dollar tip for the housekeeper when most folks leave only a couple bucks."

They thanked the woman and headed back to the car. Once they were inside, Sawyer turned to her, his eyes flashing. "I know where he is. Well, not exactly where. But I have a good idea where to look. One place where you can work for room and board and a small salary is a ranch. Those little cowboy hats meant more than I realized last night. He must have gotten himself a job as a ranch hand. No wonder the guy who skipped out on two months' rent is suddenly leaving tips for the housekeeper—he feels flush right now because he has a job and a place to live."

"That makes total sense," she said. "But there have to be hundreds of ranches in Wedlock Creek and environs. What's the plan to find him? Call and ask if there's a Cole Wolfe there?"

"To start," he said, reaching for his phone.

A half hour later and still in the lot of the RiverView Cabins, they'd learned he wasn't employed at the Triple C or the Dowling Ranch, two of the biggest operations in Wedlock Creek. Sawyer called another large ranch, Great Bear Ranch, forty minutes away—no Cole Wolfe there.

"Maybe he's working a small ranch or farm, one of two or three hands," Sawyer said. "That actually sounds more his speed and more on the down low."

But before Sawyer could even make a list of small ranches, Sergeant Theo Stark called requesting backup with strategy for a string of burglaries, and since Sawyer had been scarce around the department the past several days, he wanted to go in again.

"I'll make a list of possibilities," he said. "And we can check out some ranches tomorrow. If your parents or sister don't mind watching the twins again."

"I'm sure they won't. When we were leaving, I heard my mom say that Jenna was going to be so jealous that they got to babysit the twins."

"Thank God for your family," he said.

Maddie hoped he took his own statement to heart. Sawyer Wolfe might think the MacLeods were outliers in the family dependability department, but all he had to do was look at himself in how he was stepping up with the twins—and looking for his brother now.

She wouldn't point that out just yet. He might just realize it himself.

Sawyer spent a few hours at work, strategizing on the burglary case with Theo Stark and dealing with yet another complaint against Annie Potterowski's food-swiping beagle. It was close to five, so he decided to head over to the community center and see if Jake Russtower was there.

He was.

After a short orientation with the director on volunteering with the kids and introductions to the group and other volunteers, Sawyer headed out into the big main room. There was a section for basketball, a homework-studying station with cubbies and chairs, a lounge area with shelving units stacked with books, games and puzzles, where some kids were stretched out and talking, and a "track" around the perimeter, which no one was making use of at the moment. Sawyer glanced around for Jake. Short for his age and skinny, with auburn hair and dark brown eyes, he was easy to spot. He was sitting by himself on the bleachers, not particularly watching anything. He looked kind of miserable.

Sawyer grabbed a basketball and went to sit next to him. "Hey, I'm Sawyer, one of the new volunteers here. Want a play a game of one-on-one?"

Jake looked over at Sawyer for a moment, his expression bored. "What's the point? I never make a basket."

"Maybe you just need to perfect your shot," Sawyer said.

The kid all but rolled his eyes.

"Come on. I'll go first," Sawyer said, giving the ball a bounce on the bleacher below. "No one misses more shots than I do."

"Well, you just met me."

Sawyer laughed, and the boy actually smiled. Score! Without even shooting.

Jake trailed him to the hoop, and Sawyer bounced the ball a few times, eyeing the basket, hoping he wouldn't make it in on some fluke—he truly stunk. He shot and missed. Sawyer chased after the ball and bounced it to Jake, who aimed and missed.

"Try standing dead center of the hoop and fling it up with a little more gusto," Sawyer said. "And believe that you're gonna make the shot. That's key. *Believe.*"

"You could try that too," Jake clapped back.

Sawyer smiled. "Oh, I will."

Jake repositioned himself, and if Sawyer wasn't mistaken, he closed his eyes for a second to talk himself into scoring the basket. He threw—and it went in! *Thank you, universe.* "Yeah!" Jake shouted.

"Awesome!" Sawyer said. He got the ball and bounced it back to Jake, who threw again and got it in again.

"This is nuts. I never make a basket. Now I made two?"

Sawyer nodded. "You believed you could. I'm telling you, works almost every time."

"Guess it must."

"Have a hoop at home?" Sawyer asked, hoping Jake would open up a little.

"Are you kidding? That would be too loud 'for the baby.'" He scrunched up his face in disgust. "The baby, the baby. I'm so sick of what I can't do because of 'the baby,'" he added in a singsong voice.

"New baby brother or sister?" Sawyer asked.

"Brother. *Half* brother. My dad remarried. And before you ask, let's just get it out of the way because I don't want to talk about it. My mom is dead. She died three years ago in a car accident. Okay?"

"We have a lot in common. My mom died when I was young too. And my dad also had a baby when I was a kid. I was five when my half brother was born."

Jake stared at Sawyer, his mouth slightly hanging open. "Really?"

"Yup," Sawyer said, bouncing the ball and aiming—and missing.

Jake ran down the ball, which meant Sawyer had him on his side. "Try again," he said, bouncing the ball to Sawyer.

Sawyer shot. And missed.

Jake's brown eyes lit up with glee. "Wow, you weren't kidding. I'm kind of amazed you taught me the secrets to getting it in when you can't do it yourself."

"The rules of making the shot apply to most things in life. Center yourself. Believe. Go for it."

Jake shrugged.

"You and your stepmom close?" Sawyer asked, shooting again. And missing.

"I can't stand her even if she's nice most of the time. She's always telling me what to do. So what if I want to eat a bag of Cheetos for dinner? Who cares? And then I argue back why I should be able to, and my dad gets mad. Oh yeah, living in my house is a lot of fun."

His parents seemed to care about him. Jake was clearly lonely, feeling left out of his family because of the new baby, and didn't seem to have friends. Other kids were in pairs or groups, but Jake had been sitting alone.

"Jake!" a voice called.

"Oh, great," Jake muttered. "It's my dad. We'll have, like, five seconds together on the way to the car where my stepmother and the infant from hell are. And then I'll be yelled at if I breathe too loud."

Sawyer smiled. "Get along with your dad?"

"Sometimes. But all he cares about is stupid dumb Amy and stupid dumb Dylan the brat."

Vince Russtower began walking over, then seemed to recognize Sawyer out of uniform and stopped dead in his tracks. He looked nervous as he approached. "Jake in trouble?"

"Why would I be in trouble?" Jake asked, frowning. "Why do you always think I'm doing something wrong?"

"Because you're standing with the chief of police," Vince told his son. "That's why."

Jake's mouth fully dropped open. "You're a cop? The top cop?"

"I am. Sawyer Wolfe." He extended his hand, and Jake at first didn't seem to know what to do with it, then reached out to shake it. Sawyer turned to Vince. "Vince Russtower, right?"

He caught the slight rise of the man's eyebrow. "Yeah." He had the feeling from Russtower's expression that he didn't want his son to know that his father had had dealings with the police before.

"Nice to meet you," Sawyer said.

Vince's shoulders relaxed. "You too." He turned to Jake. "Ready? Where's your backpack?"

Jake jogged over to the bleachers to get it.

"Nice kid," Sawyer said. "I just started volunteering with the kids."

Vince nodded, and Jake joined them again. Vince took the backpack on his own shoulder and said, "Well, Amy and Dylan are waiting, so let's get going, Jake."

"Thanks for practicing with me," Jake said to Sawyer.

"I'll be here every other weekday from five to six p.m.," Sawyer said. "Catch you next time."

They walked away, and when they reached the door, Jake turned back to look at Sawyer. Sawyer held up a hand and so did Jake, then they were gone.

He let out a breath. That kid reminded him a lot of himself.

Another boy was now sitting by himself on the floor, so Sawyer went over to him and asked if he wanted to shoot. The kid jumped up and said "Sure!" with a big smile.

And put one on Sawyer's face too. Coming here had been a good idea, and he wished he'd done it long ago.

If he hadn't made Maddie feel she couldn't tell him about her own volunteer work with babies, he might have been inspired to offer himself to the community center kids' group years ago. He might have wanted to give back in that way, too, but he'd been so rough with her dream, her fondest wish, that she didn't even want to share with him that she was working with babies at the hospital.

He wished he could change so much about the past. But at least he could work on the future.

And the now.

Chapter Ten

While Max still napped, Maddie held Shane in her arms in his soft green pajamas and showed him the Christmas tree by the window in the living room. "Ooh, look at all the sparkly white lights and the pretty silver star. And these are our ornaments. See the *M* for *Max* and *S* for *Shane*? Okay, fine, it's really *M* for *Maddie* and *S* for *Sawyer*, but now we get to share initials! And there's the Woodstock ornament your uncle Sawyer gave me for Christmas when we were thirteen—"

She remembered that! She waited a beat for more to come, but nothing did. She simply had remembered when she'd gotten the ornament and from whom, but there was no accompanying images in her mind. Too bad. She wanted to remember her childhood, which sounded pretty wonderful.

She was moving around the tree to show Shane the hand-painted little globe ornament with a photo of Moose on it when she recalled something else. She saw herself sitting in a cozy room on a tan velvet sofa, Sawyer sitting beside her, leaning back while she sat forward. A middle-aged woman she didn't recognize sitting in an ornate chair across from them.

You do have a choice, Maddie, the woman said. *You could accept that Sawyer doesn't want children, something he has always stated and has not wavered on. Or you could not accept it and hope, as you have been, that he will eventually change his mind.*

She must be remembering an appointment with the marriage counselor. Beyond the woman were two arched windows, snow falling gently. It was only December, so this appointment had to be recent.

But both are impossible choices, Maddie said. *I can't bear the former and the latter is killing me.*

The counselor looked at her, then at Sawyer, then back at Maddie. *Another choice is leaving the marriage.*

Maddie gasped. *I don't want to leave Sawyer. I don't want a divorce. I love him!*

Then maybe you need to accept that you're not going to have children, the counselor said.

But why does he get to make that choice for me? If he can make that choice for me, I should be able to make the choice for him—that we're having a baby, end of story.

He's the one saying no, that's why.

So I'm supposed to stay in this marriage and what? Resent him? Watch my sister live my dream?

Sawyer, the counselor said. *Would you like to say something?*

Maddie looked at him. He was tense, his expression grim.

I don't want to lose my wife. But I don't want children.

Broken record! Maddie heard herself scream.

Sawyer dropped his head in his hands.

Maybe you should think about a separation, the counselor said. *To see what it feels like.*

What the hell? Sawyer snapped, bolting up and storming out.

The memory faded to nothing. She wasn't in the counselor's office anymore. She didn't see herself rushing after Sawyer. But he'd told her what happened afterward.

That was clearly right before the accident. She closed her eyes, cradling Shane gently in her arms, grateful to have this precious little being to hold. The memory she'd just had felt so strange out of context, on its own, without the before. She did have the after, though.

She'd felt her frustration on that sofa. Her disappointment and anger. Her helplessness in her own life. She'd hated how she'd felt in that office, like she was jumping out of her skin, unable to direct her own life, unable to make her dream come true because of the roadblock called her husband.

Whom she loved. Maddie knew in that snatch of memory that she'd never considered leaving Sawyer, that she didn't want a baby *more* than she wanted to be with her husband. *Therein lies the damned rub*, she thought, shaking her head.

"I'm glad I don't remember it all," she whispered to Shane. "Sounds really hard. No—it sounds impossible."

Shane gazed up at her with his slate-blue eyes, bow lip quirking like Billy Idol's, which made her smile. The lip quirked again, and she full-out laughed. *What would we do without you and your brother?* she thought, kissing his sweet little head. The two Wolfe boys had brought joy and purpose and direction to her life since the accident—and hopefully showed Sawyer another side of himself.

She heard Sawyer's key in the lock. She came into the entryway with Shane as Sawyer was taking off his down jacket, his impressive body never failing to catch her off guard and take her attention and breath for a moment.

"Everything okay today?" he asked, closing the closet door. "C'mere you little rascal," he added, reaching for Shane.

He adored the babies. If he didn't, he

would give the baby a brief smile and walk right past them into a kitchen for a drink or the living room to relax. But he wanted to hold Shane. Yup, the twins had gotten to him.

Because they're not his? Not here to stay?

Something occurred to her just then. If Cole never came back for his children, and the babies *were* here to stay, was Sawyer able to handle that notion better because they weren't his children? They were his nephews. She frowned, turning that over in her mind.

"Everything was great." She handed the baby to him, her jumble of thoughts obliterated by the loving way Sawyer gently cradled Shane in his arms, careful of his neck, giving him a kiss on his fuzzy head. "Although I did have a vivid memory of that final counseling session. It ended with you storming out. I remembered a very long stretch of the conversation, including the counselor suggesting the separation. Then I was back to being blank."

He looked at her, his smile fading. "That session was brutal. On both of us."

"But necessary, I think," she said. "The counselor laid out the facts."

"And we didn't know what to do with them."

Exactly, Maddie thought. "Which is why the counselor went nuclear with the separation suggestion. To get us to take another step forward instead of remaining stagnant. But I guess time ended up standing still in a different way once I lost my memory."

He nodded and seemed uncomfortable. "Max sleeping?"

Yup. Uncomfortable. Enough to change the subject. "Yeah. He'll probably wake up any minute. Then we can feed them."

"Why don't you go relax," he said.

"I've got the twins. You had them alone all day."

I don't want to relax. I want to spend time with you. But Sawyer seemed to want some space between them when they'd had space from each other the past several hours.

Then again, she wouldn't mind a hot soothing bath where she could think. And not about the fact that Sawyer seemed to be trying to avoid her right now.

The doorbell rang, and Maddie turned around on the stairwell and went to answer it, since Sawyer had the baby in his arms.

She opened the door and gasped.

Cole Wolfe stood on the porch.

At Maddie's gasp, Sawyer turned around to find his brother standing in the doorway, his gaze on the baby in Sawyer's arms.

His instinct was to turn and protect Shane, but he fought it. "Cole."

"Can I come in?" Cole asked, digging his hands in his pockets. He wore the black leather jacket he'd had for years, and a thin plaid scarf around his neck. His jeans were worn at the knees and scuffed with dirt. Sawyer would put money on his brother having a job as a ranch hand.

"Of course," Maddie said, gesturing for him to enter and closing the door behind him.

All Sawyer had wanted yesterday and over the past several days was for Cole to call or text, or for him and Maddie to find the guy. Suddenly he was here, in the flesh, and Sawyer wanted him gone.

Why?

Because you don't trust him—and not with the twins, who are reliant on dependable people to have their every need met. That's why. Made sense to Sawyer. So then why had he been trying to find

Cole? To talk to him about what? To find out what? There was no way he could imagine Cole walking out of this house with Shane and Max; the guy was completely unprepared to care for them.

Yet you couldn't stop staring at your phone, waiting for him to call or text—and return, he knew.

What exactly did you want to happen? Do you want to happen?

Here he was again, off-kilter, unsure of what was going on inside him.

"Which one is that?" Cole asked, and if Sawyer wasn't mistaken, his brother's eyes brimmed with tears. Cole dropped his head and closed his eyes. "I don't even know which baby that is. And he's my son. I'm so pathetic."

"Cole, honey," Maddie said, "if we didn't always put Shane in green and Max in blue, we wouldn't be able to tell them apart so easily either. Old trick my experienced-with-twins mom taught us."

"Shane has slightly sharper features than Max," Sawyer said.

Cole nodded and craned his neck to peer at the baby.

Oh, hell. Sawyer walked closer to his brother. "He's a good baby. A little more demanding than Max, but a champion napper and snuggler. He likes being held."

"When I held them in the hospital, one at a time," Cole said, "I kept being afraid I'd drop them on their heads."

Sawyer nodded. "I get it. They do seem pretty fragile, but they're hardy little guys." He eyed Cole, suspicion clawing at him. Why was he here? To see the twins? Make sure they were all right, because he cared? To take them?

About that last one: over Sawyer's dead body.

Thing was, as the chief of police, no one knew better than Sawyer that Cole had every right to walk right out of here with the twins.

"Would you like to hold him?" Maddie asked Cole.

"I don't know," Cole said, shifting from foot to foot. "I don't think so. I'm just—I don't know what I am."

"Well, why don't you start by explaining why you're here," Sawyer said.

Maddie shot him a look. *Dial it down.*

Cole stared at Shane in Sawyer's arms. "Because they're here." Again, tears shone in his eyes, and Sawyer felt his guard both go down and back up. Up and down, down and up. Just like his relationship with Cole over the years.

"What do you want to happen, Cole?" Sawyer asked. "Be honest."

Cole dropped down onto the bottom step, scrubbing a hand over his face. "I don't know." He let out a breath, his eyes closed. "I have children. I made children. That baby you're holding is my son. Ever since I left them here, I kept saying that in my head—my sons, my sons. And those words never sounded remotely possible."

Maddie reached out a hand to Cole's shoulder. "I can understand how you feel."

"Who abandons their own kids?" Cole asked, his voice broken. "The worst of the worst. My dad, for example."

Sawyer felt that one straight to the heart. *Cripes, this is complicated.* On so many levels.

"You didn't abandon them," Maddie said, sitting beside him on the step. "You brought them here, where you knew they'd be well taken care of until you got your head together."

Cole looked at her. "You were always way too nice, Maddie."

That was true. And not just where Cole was concerned.

"I got a job as a ranch hand at the Johannsen place. Just me and another guy and the family. I muck out stalls and they're teaching me other stuff, like grooming. Stuff I'm very interested in. When I got that job, I felt like I had a chance, you know? Like I'm where I belong and can make a place."

Sawyer might have congratulated himself for being right about the job on a ranch if he wasn't so stuck on what Cole had just said. "A place for...?" Sawyer prompted. Maddie shot him another look. *Give him some breathing room.* But Sawyer needed to know what his brother was planning. "You can't mean raising infants in a bunkhouse? Who's going to watch them while you're mucking out stalls?"

"I just mean..." Cole's shoulders slumped. "I don't know what I mean."

"Well, how about this, Cole?" Maddie said, sliding a glance at Sawyer before focusing on his brother. "Why don't you visit with Shane and Max right now for a bit, and then you'll head back to the ranch and you'll come here tomorrow for dinner. How does that sound for an immediate plan?"

Cole perked up some. "Sounds good. What time tomorrow?"

"Let's say seven. Good, Sawyer?"

Sawyer nodded. He supposed. A brief visit tonight, dinner tomorrow. Small steps. That actually sounded just right. A cry came from the living room, and they all turned toward the sound.

"There's our cue to go get Max," Sawyer said.

Cole and Maddie stood and they all headed into the living room. Maddie went to the bassinet across from the Christmas tree and scooped out Max, who was flailing his skinny little arm.

"Is he sick?" Cole asked, worry in his eyes.

"Probably just hungry," Sawyer said. "Or wet. Or lonely. Or wants to be vertical."

"Or all the above," Maddie said. "Sawyer, why don't you let Cole hold Shane while you change Max. I'll go make their bottles."

Cole bit his lip and took a step back. "Sure I won't drop him?"

"Just don't," Sawyer said. "Keep your attention on him and you'll do fine."

Maddie sent him a smile as she went into the kitchen.

"How do I take him?" Cole asked, stepping closer.

"Put your arms out like mine are," Sawyer said. "Make sure you support his neck with your hand or forearm. That's vital until their neck muscles get stronger. You said you held the babies in the hospital, right?"

"Yeah. For almost an hour. I tried to keep it even between them, but I think I held one longer."

Sawyer smiled. "We've been trying to keep things even too. Doesn't always work out, though. Max likes his sleep, so

Shane gets more stories and back rubs while I pace the nursery."

Cole eyed him. "You been doing a lot of pacing?"

"What do you think?" Sawyer asked, but this tone was a lot gentler that it had been earlier. He transferred Shane into Cole's arms, and Cole sucked in a breath and then sat down very slowly and carefully on the sofa. His gaze never left his son's face.

Sawyer wasn't sure what he'd expected this evening to be like, but it wasn't this. He'd never seen Cole so...vulnerable. Then again, yes, he had. Many times when Cole was a kid. And even sometimes as an adult—when Sawyer was patient enough to truly pay attention to the underpinnings of what was going on with Cole.

Complicated.

Max let out another wail, and Sawyer

grabbed the basket of baby stuff from under the coffee table and set it down beside the carrier on the rug, then took out Max. He laid him down on the mat and changed him, aware that Cole's eyes were on him.

"You make it look so easy," Cole said. "I'm sure I'd put the diaper on upside down or backward."

"I think I did, too, the first time," Sawyer admitted with a smile. He really had, actually. With Max changed, Sawyer scooped him up and sat down on the other side of the sofa.

"I'm sorry for just leaving the way I did," Cole said, staring straight ahead now.

"You talking to me or them?"

Cole glanced at Sawyer. "All of you. I am sorry. I was just freaking out. In a panic."

"I know." But what now? *You're visiting*

tonight, coming for dinner tomorrow and then what? Sawyer usually didn't need to have his life mapped out for him, but he didn't like the not knowing, the vague quality about all this. There was a big maybe about a very vital issue. And Sawyer didn't like it.

Maddie came into the living room with two bottles. She sat between the brothers, handing a bottle to Sawyer and then turning toward Cole with the other one. "Here you go. You just hold it angled up, and he'll drink."

Cole took the bottle and hesitated. "What if he drinks too much at once and it pours down his throat too fast?"

"Can't happen," Maddie assured him. "Max controls the flow by sucking on the nipple. Give it a try."

Cole brought the bottle to Max's lips and angled it as Maddie had said.

"A little higher," Maddie said, tipping up the bottle a bit.

"He's drinking!" Cole exclaimed, looking at Maddie and Sawyer for a moment, then back down at his son.

Sawyer sighed inwardly. Something told him Cole was just too much of a kid, despite being twenty-seven, to be anyone's dad, let alone twin newborns. He might be wrong. And yeah, baby care was brand-new to Cole, and who was to say he wouldn't pick it up and be a master at it. Times two. Could happen.

Except Sawyer didn't see it. Because he was a cynical, world-weary cop? Or because he was realistic and called it as he saw it?

Or because he didn't want it to be true?

"You're doing it just right, Cole," Maddie said with a warm smile.

"How do I know when he's done?" Cole asked. "Will he drink the whole bottle?"

"When he's done or if he needs to burp," Maddie explained, "he'll stop suckling or pause longer between suckles. You'll be able to see it."

"I think he's done," Cole said, removing the bottle and putting it onto the coffee table. Max gazed up at Cole, seemingly satisfied with the world.

"Now slip a hand under his neck and bring him up to your chest, holding him vertically, and gently pat his back so he can burp."

It took Cole a good few minutes to do that, but he managed it, widening his eyes at Maddie and Sawyer. He gave Max a few pats, and the baby let out a giant burp. Cole burst out laughing. "I did it!" Cole said. "Champion burper," he added. He looked at Maddie. "Now what do I do?"

"You can hold him upright or along your arm, a little of both, so he's not always one way. He'll let you know when he wants to be shifted. Babies love to squirm or cry with displeasure."

Cole smiled. "He seems pretty happy right now."

"Sure does," Maddie agreed.

Cole glanced around the living room, his gaze stopping on the double bassinets, the baby swings, the baskets of baby paraphernalia. "There are some events at the rodeo I'm thinking of signing up for," he said. "It would bring in a good amount of money."

"Except you don't want to do anything that would risk injury," Sawyer pointed out. "Because of the physical nature of your job, you need to be in top shape. And you've got these two to consider."

"Bronc-riding prize is a good one," Cole said. "And I'm pretty good."

"Takes one time to get injured," Sawyer said, his tone sharp.

"Says the guy who risks his life every day for a living," Cole said.

Sawyer brought Shane up to his chest and patted his back. "I'm not anyone's dad."

"You're someone's husband," Cole said, glaring at Sawyer.

A red hot pool of anger swirled in Sawyer's belly. He got up and walked with Shane over to the window, looking out. *Whatever you want to snap back at him, don't. Just shut up. He'll be gone in five minutes anyway.*

And back tomorrow for dinner.

Sawyer let out a breath.

"Cole, can I ask you something personal?" Maddie said.

What was this? He turned around, his gaze on his wife.

"I guess," Cole said.

"I'm curious about the names you chose for your sons. Max and Shane. Did you name them after anyone?"

Sawyer walked back over to the sofa and sat down. He was curious about that too. Maybe it was just a coincidence that the initials matched his and Maddie's.

"Yeah, I did," Cole said. "The two best people I know." He didn't look at Sawyer or Maddie and seemed kind of embarrassed, which told Cole the initials were no coincidence. "I named them for you and Sawyer," he added, looking over at his brother for a moment.

All the ire that had been in Sawyer's stomach a few moments ago dissipated, and something like compassion took its place. Something else, too, that Sawyer couldn't quite put his finger on. He'd never get a handle on his brother—who he was, really, what he was made of.

No one is all this or all that, he reminded himself. But it made it easier to box up Cole if he were.

"That's beautiful," Maddie said. "Thank you. We're very touched, both of us."

"You touched, Sawyer?" Cole asked with a bit of the glare still in his expression.

"I thought it was nice," Sawyer said. "Meaningful. That's a better word."

Cole looked at him and nodded. "Good." He stood up slowly. "Well, I should get back. I said I'd do some extra chores in the barn at night for overtime." He gestured toward Maddie as though he wanted to hand the baby over, and Maddie took Max. Cole headed toward the door as if he couldn't wait to get the hell out of there.

It was a lot, he'd give his brother that. Sawyer well remembered the first night the twins had been here, and he hadn't exactly known what he was doing himself.

Maddie and Sawyer, babies in their arms, followed Cole to the door. He opened the closet and got his jacket and scarf, shrugging them on.

"See you tomorrow at seven for dinner," Cole said, then took another look at Shane and Max and hurried out.

A moment later, Sawyer could hear the annoying muffler roaring to life. "At least he'll be able to get that fixed now," he said.

"Sawyer Wolfe, is that all you have to say?" Maddie snapped, one eyebrow up high.

"There's a whole history between me and Cole you don't remember," he said, then regretted it instantly. That wasn't exactly her fault. *Cripes.*

"What matters is right now and the future," she pointed out.

He nodded slowly. She was right—to a point. The whole picture mattered, just as it mattered within their marriage.

He just had no idea what was going to happen. And it was killing him.

Chapter Eleven

They'd both made themselves scarce the rest of the evening, Sawyer in his study, stewing—or at least that was what Maddie thought he was doing—and Maddie organizing her closet, then cleaning the bathroom, then remaking the already made bed.

Finally, she'd exhausted herself. She'd already been wiped out mentally from Cole's unexpected visit, and now she was physically zonked too. She slipped into bed, pulled up the comforter under her neck and stared at the ceiling, wondering if Sawyer would be coming up anytime soon. Probably more like after 1:00 a.m. when he figured she'd be asleep.

Forget that noise, she thought, a little adrenaline racing as she got out of bed, stuffed her feet into her furry slippers and went downstairs to find her husband.

She stopped dead in her tracks in the doorway of his study. He was sitting in his desk chair, back toward the door, flipping through photos on his computer—of himself and Cole. One filled the screen of him and Cole as young adults, making cannonballs into a lake or river.

Sawyer could be hardheaded, but the man wasn't hard-hearted. His brother meant a lot to him, problems and all, and instead of focusing on the bad times, he was clearly immersing himself in the good ones.

"Hey," she said softly, the ire completely out of her.

He turned around. "Hi. I was just going back in time, I guess."

"You two had some really nice moments, from the looks of the photos."

"Few and far between," he said. "But yeah. Like this one."

She walked over and put her hands on the chair back, peering at the photo. "Did I take that?"

"Yup. The water was cold so you didn't want to go in, but Cole and I dared each other. And of course we couldn't just dive in."

She smiled. "You okay?"

He gave something of a shrug, and she leaned closer to massage his shoulders. "Oh, that feels good. Thank you."

She kept massaging, loving the feel of his strong shoulders and thinking about the other night when they'd been so drawn to each other that they'd made love against their better judgment.

"I can't see Cole as a full-time father,"

he said, letting his head drop back. "Can you?"

"With time, maybe. He does seem very far from that. But necessity is the mother of invention, isn't that what they say?"

"For some people. For others, people like Cole, necessity means taking off to avoid responsibility."

She felt a knot in his left shoulder and kneaded a bit on that spot. "But he does seem to be trying, at least. He put care into finding this job, something he's passionate about, too, and one that comes with room and board. He's working, trying to build something for himself—and very likely, the twins."

"That build is going to be a while, though. He's not taking the twins for a long time, Maddie. In fact, I'd say years. Maybe never."

She stopped massaging and turned his chair around to face her. "And how do you feel about that?"

"I'd rather those boys I've come to care very deeply about are with people who will raise them with everything they need."

"And what's that?" she asked.

"Devotion. Commitment. Responsibility. We're a solid family in a solid home."

Except a week ago we were on the verge of separating.

She glanced at the photo, then back at Sawyer. "I think he wants to turn his life around and become a dad. That's the sense I got. But you're right that I don't have the full picture. I don't remember how he's behaved in the past. What you said about stealing from us? Taking my grandmother's bracelet? That's pretty bad." She could only imagine how that had hurt Sawyer, what it had cost him to harden himself the way he had after— Cole had finally crossed a line for Sawyer.

He nodded. "It's possible that having

children, being a father got to him. But wanting to change and changing are very different things."

"Let's go up to bed," she said, reaching out her hand. "I was exhausted before I came down, and now I might fall asleep on the floor in here right now."

She was so glad she had come down after him instead of wondering and worrying by herself in bed or pulling the covers over her head. Now they'd talked and she felt better and was sure he did too.

He smiled and stood and wrapped her in a hug. He smelled delicious. She could stay like this all night—and would, if he'd carry her and she could sleep in his arms.

Upstairs, she got back into bed, and when he emerged from the bathroom in a T-shirt and sweats, he looked so incredibly sexy.

"Think I was too hard on him?" he asked.

"I don't know. A little. Or maybe not.

Maybe he needs someone being tough on him. Someone he knows cares. You heard what he said. We're the best people he knows." She smiled, recalling the reverence in Cole's voice as he'd said it.

Sawyer got into bed beside her, his gaze on the ceiling, hands behind his head. "He says stuff like that, and for half a second, it wipes away all the bad. I forget the theft, the lies. And then he turns around and ruins it five minutes later."

"He did okay tonight. I thought he was sincere."

He turned onto his side, propping his head on his elbow. "Seemed so. I don't know. I can't see him taking the twins anytime soon."

"You sound kind of glad about that," she said, facing him. "Are you?"

"They belong with us, Maddie. He's not remotely prepared to care for them. Not now or the immediate future."

"People *can* change."

"I didn't," he blurted out and then froze for a second as he seemed to realize he wasn't doing himself any favors.

He hadn't changed his position in seven years of marriage. He didn't want children. But he seemed comfortable with the idea of permanently keeping the twins.

Why?

She stared at him, feeling her eyes narrowing to slits as a thought occurred to her.

"You're comfortable keeping the twins because they're your nephews," she said. "Yes. That's it, isn't it? They're not your children. There'll always be that line there. So you're able to deal. Oh, and I get to be the 'mom' I've always wanted to be."

He tensed, moving onto his back and staring at the ceiling again, his hands folded over his chest.

She sat up. "Do I have that right?"

She knew she did.

"It's complicated, Maddie. I don't have all the answers right now. And everything is very new."

"Now you sound like Cole. Not okay for him but okay for you?"

He grabbed his pillow and walked out of the room.

Maddie turned onto her side and stared at her Woodstock alarm clock.

She wondered how many nights they'd slept in separate rooms. Those memories hadn't come back yet. But now she had a fresh one.

If you have to be stubborn at your own expense, that's bad enough, Sawyer remembered April MacLeod saying a time or two over the years. *But being stubborn at others' expense and taking them down with you? No good.*

He'd heard his mother-in-law's raspy voice in his head as he lay on the sofa in the living room, the throw barely big enough to cover up to his chest, Moose on the floor beside him. It had gotten him off the couch and back up the stairs not ten minutes after stomping down. Maddie didn't deserve this kind of treatment, him stalking off with his pillow because she was being too honest for him.

When he'd gotten into bed next to her and spooned against her, wondering if she'd shift away from him, he'd been relieved when she'd taken his hand and held it tightly.

"We love each other and we'll figure it all out," he'd whispered, then mentally kicked himself for saying something he's said at least twenty times the past year. Even if Maddie couldn't remember any of those times, she also deserved better than platitudes, but right then he'd been unable to come up with answers to her earlier questions.

Was she right? He was okay with raising the twins—and he *was* okay with that—because they *weren't* his children? He'd wanted to say, *If I'm raising them, they're mine. Just like they're yours*, but he knew what Maddie had meant, even if he couldn't articulate the difference. Did the word *nephews* make it possible for Sawyer to create an emotional distance between the twins and himself?

The morning didn't bring clarity either. Maddie was out of the room when he woke up, the bright sun barely blocked by the curtains. He listened for the sound of her voice downstairs, talking to the twins as he always did, but there was silence.

He got out of bed and went downstairs and looked around. No Maddie. No twins. He headed into the kitchen, where he was sure he'd find a note leaning in front of the coffee maker—he drank a lot of coffee these days—and there it was.

Took the twins out early for breakfast with my parents and then to hang out at MacLeod's for a little while. Might do some Christmas shopping after. I'll text you. PS. I let Moose out and fed him. —M

Moose now stared at him forlornly, missing her too. Sawyer had been hoping they'd spend the day together. To try to make up for yesterday, for the way they'd argued and his immature stomp off downstairs, though he had rectified that, and she'd welcomed him back with one squeeze of her hand. Maybe he should let her have a little space from him, since that was what she seemed to want this morning. They could meet up for Christmas shopping, since he wanted to buy for the family he'd "adopted" for Christmas, getting everything on their list and a whole lot more, plus start looking around at bicycles for Jake. Tonight, before the dinner with Cole, he'd volunteer at the community center and surreptitiously find out what kind of bike he wanted and what color.

He poured himself a cup of the coffee

Maddie had thoughtfully made, the silence in the house bugging him. It was too quiet. He used to like the quiet, grateful that Moose wasn't much of a barker unless he was alerting. But since two tiny humans had come into his life, his and Maddie's lives, their cries and shrieks had come to sound like music to him. He liked caring for them, figuring out their needs and meeting them. There was something satisfying about it.

Because of what Maddie had theorized—and it was just that, a theory—about being able to handle the thought of taking on the twins permanently because he had the buffer of uncle?

Maybe.

He didn't really want to think about that, so he took the stairs two at a time, showered, dressed in his uniform and drove to the PD. He conquered the mound of paperwork in his inbox, went out on a call with his rookie, Mobley, and strategized on a difficult case with sergeant Theo Stark.

He glanced at Theo's desk, the attached four photo frames containing pictures of his quadruplet toddlers, Tyler, Henry, Ethan and Olivia. Last Christmas, Theo had shocked everyone by the fact that he wasn't dead, after all. Supposedly killed in an explosion on the job, he'd faked his death to protect his wife, who'd been threatened by the mobster he'd been after. Theo had had no idea his wife had been pregnant with quads—and when he finally came back, they were barely a year old. The man Sawyer had known then had lived and breathed his job, taking the most dangerous cases, but he'd given all that up to devote himself more fully to his family. Sawyer hadn't been the chief back then; he'd been promoted when the former chief had retired soon after, so he didn't know all the personal details. But Theo had gone from a guy he'd call a real lone wolf to a family man. And Sawyer wanted to know how. He and Theo were around the same age, and he'd always sensed a kindred spirit in the guy.

"Did you always want a big family, Stark?" Sawyer asked, his gaze on the photos.

Theo laughed. "I didn't want a family at all. But one was waiting for me when I finally came home. I had no idea how great it is."

"Kids?"

"The whole thing. A family. My wife—Allie. The quads. Sunday dinner with her family. Toddler classes. Nap time. Bath time. Story time. Colds and skinned knees. Sibling rivalry. I love it all. End of the day, I can't wait to get home to all that."

Sawyer raised an eyebrow. "What changed for you?"

"I guess I was hanging on to some baggage like a lot of people do. The quads forced my hand in letting go. My wife helped too." He smiled. "I was an idiot for a long time. I'm glad I'm not anymore."

Huh. He glanced at the photos again. He recalled hearing that the quads had been named for Theo—each one taking an initial. Tyler, Henry, Ethan, Olivia. That had choked up quite a few of them when they'd first learned Allie Stark was expecting quads and was going to name them after the "fallen" officer. He thought about Cole filling out the birth certificate application and deciding to name the babies after him and Maddie. He knew that meant a lot, but now that he really thought about it, he got kind of choked up himself.

"Things going okay with watching your brother's newborns?" Theo asked. "I'm full of tips if you need any."

"Thanks. I have to say, things are going better than I thought. You just do what needs to be done, and sometimes it's that easy."

Theo nodded. "Exactly. And plus, those little sneaks steal your heart without you even realizing it. One day, you just realize you're completely controlled by your devotion to people who weigh less than thirty pounds."

Sawyer laughed. "Or in my case, less than fifteen pounds combined."

"Happens that fast," Theo said with a smile. His phone rang, so Sawyer headed back to his desk.

His own phone pinged with a text. Jenna invited Maddie and the twins over, so she was skipping shopping today and would see him at home later.

He frowned. He wanted to be with her right now. Wanted to see the twins, hold them.

She pinged back a second later.

Oh, you know what I was thinking? Wouldn't it be nice if you talked to Cole about volunteering at the community center with you? You could spend some time with him, and he could spend some time around kids. Win-win.

Except that Sawyer and Cole couldn't seem to be in each other's company for more than ten minutes without biting each other's heads off. And Cole—volunteering? He couldn't see it.

He glanced at the time. Four thirty. He needed to be at the community center at five for his shift. He thought about Jake Russtower, and how Sawyer had told him they had a lot in common. He also thought about Jake asking him one day if he and his own half brother were close, and Sawyer having to say no, that they barely spoke, let alone got along.

Maybe if he and Cole volunteered together, it would say something to Jake, show him something. And maybe he and Cole would have something else in common besides a rocky history.

296 A WYOMING CHRISTMAS TO REMEMBER

Score a zillion for Maddie.

He pulled out his phone and texted Cole with the info.

Interested? he added.

I guess, Cole texted back. Predictably. He always guessed.

Jeez, lighten up on him, will ya? he heard Maddie say inside his head.

Which made him smile. What he would do without Maddie he really didn't know. Didn't want to know.

Okay, I can be there by 5:15, Cole wrote back.

See you then, Sawyer texted and put his phone back into his pocket.

So they'd volunteer together, then Cole would come home with him for dinner. That was a long stretch of time. Without Maddie to run interference.

Chapter Twelve

"Want to shoot some hoops?" Sawyer asked as he walked over to where Jake sat on the bleachers—alone again. The boy wore a gray hoodie and dark jeans, his mop of reddish-brown hair falling into his eyes.

"No." Jake stared straight ahead.

Sawyer sat down beside him. "Something on your mind?"

Jake shrugged. Sawyer knew that classic move well. It said, *Yes, but talking about it is hard for me.*

"I'm not great at basketball, but I've been told I'm a good listener." He kept his gaze straight ahead instead of crowding the boy by looking at him.

Jake frowned and crossed his arms over his chest. "My dad said we'd go ice fishing—just the two of us. He promised that we would the first weekend of Christmas break. And now we're not going."

"He tell you why?"

"Because of 'the baby,'" he said in a singsong voice. "The baby, everything's about 'the baby.' Of course Amy doesn't want to take care of the brat by herself, so now my dad said we can't go."

Jake looked equal parts angry and hurt.

"I understand why you're upset," Sawyer said. "Yeah, having a new baby kind of takes over for a little while. I know because I'm watching my brother's newborns for a bit. My life is definitely not my own."

Jake chewed his bottom lip and glanced

at him. "Well, I'm sure if you wanted to take your kid ice fishing like you promised, your wife wouldn't make you cancel on him."

"I don't have any kids of my own, actually."

"So forget it," Jake said, rolling his eyes. "You don't even know what I'm talking about."

"What *are* we talking about?" a voice asked.

Sawyer turned around to find Cole standing there, dressed in jeans and his leather jacket. He nodded at Cole.

"Jake, this is my brother, Cole. I was telling you about him the other day. He's five years younger than I am."

"We have the same father, different mothers," Cole said. "Except Sawyer's the only one who got the father."

Sawyer was about to shoot Cole a look that said, *Really? That's appropriate?* But

Cole's comment did serve the purpose of perking Jake right up.

"Why?" Jake asked, sitting up straighter and tilting his head.

Cole put a foot up on the bleacher and stretched his calf muscle, then repeated with the other leg. "Our dad didn't want a second kid. One was enough. Sawyer broke the mold, I guess."

Sawyer shook his head. He was hardly the favorite. "Yeah right. Dad barely paid attention to me."

"You still grew up with him," Cole said.

"So, your dad stuck with the older kid and ignored the new one," Jake said, his dark eyes lighting up. "Interesting. Maybe there's hope for me."

"Oh, thanks," Cole said with a lazy grin. "So are we gonna stand around talking about unpleasant crud or are we going to shoot the ball?"

Jake grinned back and got up and stole the ball, dribbling it to the hoop and shooting. He missed. Cole stole it and shot—scored.

"Can you teach me how to shoot like that?" Jake asked, chasing down the ball and bouncing it to Cole.

"Just keep working on your shot," Cole said. "Find your best spot. Shoot it hard—mean it. And pop that baby in," he added, dribbling to the hoop and demonstrating all he'd said. Of course the ball went right in. "Also helps to be six inches taller."

Jake laughed. "Good point. My dad's really tall, so I think I will be too."

Sawyer stole the ball, shot—and missed.

"So what's my brother's excuse?" Cole joked. "He's six-two."

Jake loved that. "Burn!" he said, holding up his palm for a high five to Cole, which Cole delighted in receiving.

"Ha, ha," Sawyer said. "Everyone knows I'm a baseball guy."

"Uh, they do?" Cole asked, winking at Jake, who laughed again. Cole grabbed the ball and shot again and scored. "Look, Jake, if you want some one-on-one with your dad, just the two of you, I suggest you plan a sneak attack. Works in basketball, will work at home."

"I've already talked to my dad about it. All I got back was the usual whatever about 'the baby.'"

"No—the sneak attack isn't on your dad," Cole said. "He's not in control. It's the *stepmother* you need in your court." He bounced the ball for emphasis. "What you want to do is get her to see things your way. Then she makes your case for you and you get what you want."

Now that had Jake's total attention. He moved closer to Cole. "What do I say to her?"

"You say, Daphne, or whatever her name is—"

"It's Amy."

"You say, Amy, I really miss my dad. I know he has a whole new family and everything, but I don't get to spend any time with him one-on-one anymore, and maybe we can schedule something every week just me and him. Like every Monday, from five to six, he comes here and shoots hoops with me."

Jake rolled his eyes again. "Like she'd say yes. Right."

"Maybe she will," Cole said. "Especially when she knows what's in it for her."

"What could possibly be in it for her?" Jake asked.

Cole shook his bangs out of his eyes. "Two things. One, she gets to feel like she's bringing father and son closer together. Two, you'll get off her back. And a happier Jake means a happier house. Tell her you know you've been moping around and you think spending just an hour one-on-one with your dad here would really change things for you."

Jake considered that, biting his lip on a

slow nod. "They do say I sulk a lot. She might go for it."

Cole dribbled the ball, turning and bouncing the ball between his legs. "I bet she will. Ask her when you get home tonight."

Jake stole the ball. "I will," he said, shooting and scoring a three-pointer. "Yeah! My first three-pointer! The crowd goes wild!"

Cole put his hands around his mouth and made a whooshing sound.

They spent the next half hour taking turns shooting. Sawyer had no idea Cole was so good at basketball—or with kids. He made a huge impression on Jake. It also helped that he was younger than Sawyer and looked it, with his mop of hair and "whatever" attitude, which appealed to Cole. Right now, Cole was telling Jake he was a cowboy, and he had the kid rapt as he talked about the border collie who worked the ranch as an honorary cowboy, keeping the herd in line.

Cole really had a way with Jake and could do wonders here at the center.

"I went here after school every day when I was a kid," Cole said. "At first I hated it, but then I never wanted to leave. It's a good program. You come every day?"

"Yup."

"How do you get here?" Cole asked. "Bike? Biking will build up your leg muscles for fast shifts on the court."

"I walk. My bike's too small now, and my dad said they can't replace it right now unless he can find a used one. So my dad picks me up from here. Of course 'the baby' and my stepmother are usually waiting in the car, so he can never shoot hoops with me."

"I can definitely say my dad never picked me up from anywhere, ever," Cole said. "You know, I once had the best mountain bike. Huge tires, bright orange color, water-bottle holder, back rack. That bike was the best."

Sawyer stared at Cole, thinking about the comment about their dad. There was usually bitterness in Cole's voice when he talked about Hank Wolfe. But just then, he seemed more focused on Jake—and indirectly pointing out that getting picked up by your dad was pretty cool.

"That's what I would want if I could get a bike," Jake said. "A mountain bike. Either orange or silver."

Bingo. Sawyer had been planning to get some intel from Jake about the bike he'd listed as his sole Christmas want on the Holiday Happymakers form. Thanks to Cole, he got it.

"Maybe Santa will bring you a new bike," Cole said. "You never know."

"Yeah, sure. My dad can't afford it right now since 'the baby' gets everything. I wrote one of those wish lists for the

Happy Holidaymakers tree or whatever it's called but since there's no such thing as Santa, I know I'm not getting anything. My dad and Amy will probably buy me a pair of pajamas."

"I hated getting clothes as gifts as a kid," Cole agreed.

"Right?" Jake said with a knowing nod.

"Jake, time go to," Vince Russtower called from by the side door.

Cole glanced over at Vince, seemingly sizing him up. "Remember, sneak attack," he said, fist-bumping Jake.

Jake grabbed his jacket and backpack with a grin and ran over to his dad.

"Wow," Sawyer said. "You really have a way with kids. That was amazing."

Cole shrugged. "Whenever I see a sulking kid, I think of myself, I guess, and get all empathetic."

"Well, I think you made a big impression on Jake. And your advice about talking to his stepmother about needing a little time alone with his dad was a great idea."

"It should work too," Cole said. "It did on my mom, and she hated our dad. I'd tell her I was the way I was because I never got to spend any time with my dad, and she'd sigh and call him up and try to get him to make plans with me. Not that our dad ever did."

"He just wasn't a good person, Cole. It had nothing to do with you or me. He was just…limited."

Cole shrugged and scooped up the ball from where Jake had left it, scoring a three-pointer. "I hate talking about this stuff. Is it time for dinner?"

Sawyer smiled. "No, but let's go wow some other kid with your basketball skills."

Now it was Cole who smiled.

Huh. Maddie had been right again. Volunteering together had done wonders for him and Cole in just thirty minutes of throwing a ball around the makeshift court.

"Jake has it better than he knows," Cole said. "But everything's relative, isn't it? I can't imagine Dad even picking *you* up from after-school care."

"He wouldn't have. I can tell you stories about walking miles in the snow—and mean it."

Cole grinned, then his smile faded. "You still grew up with him, though. You had a dad."

"And you had a mother. I didn't."

"Not the same thing," Cole said.

"We each had one parent," Sawyer reminded him. "How is it not the same?"

"You've said that a million times. And I've told you why a million times. You got the dad, I got no dad. We didn't have the same mom. There's no equivalency."

Sawyer thought there was, but he understood what Cole meant. They shared a dad and Sawyer had lived with him, and

Cole saw him maybe five times before he graduated from high school.

"Hey, look, it's another me from elementary school," Cole said, then jogged up to the boy. He said something, and then a second later, the kid who'd been sitting alone was on the court, dribbling toward the hoop.

"You should come here as often as you can," Sawyer told his brother. "This is your thing."

Cole chased down the ball for the boy and bounced it back to him. "I did okay with Jake. I might have the answers to this little dude's issues too."

Sawyer smiled. "Talk to the director about setting up a volunteer schedule. Even twice a week would mean a lot to this place."

Cole nodded. "You think that's okay, though?"

"I think what's okay?"

Cole snagged the errant basketball with

his foot and bounced it back to the boy, who was now practicing dribbling. "Making time for coming here when..." He trailed off, biting his lip and looking at the floor.

Sawyer tilted his head, not sure what his brother meant, where he was going with this.

"Because of the twins, I mean," Cole said. "I'm gonna volunteer with kids twice a week when I don't even take care of my own?" There was a sheen in his eyes, and he turned away.

Oh, hell. "Hey," Sawyer said, putting an arm around Cole's shoulder. "It's all about building a life that allows for fatherhood. The job at the ranch. Coming here. Working on who you are in positive ways. How you were with Jake, how you got this other kid up and playing? That says a lot about the kind of father you can be, Cole."

"You think I could be a decent dad?" He looked away again, biting his lip.

"Of course I think you could be. You just have to show up. And by that I mean you have to make a commitment in your head, in here," he said, bumping Cole's chest, "that your sons come first. Once you do that, everything else falls into place."

"Dinnertime yet?" Cole asked again. "I think I'm all talked out."

Sawyer smiled. "Actually, yes."

"Hey, wait," Cole said. "I just realized I'll be going from conversations I don't want to have here to conversations I don't want to have at your house."

"But the twins are there, right? That's why you have to deal."

Cole bit his lip again. "Still doesn't feel real. They don't feel like mine, Sawyer. Is that weird?"

"I don't know. They feel like *mine*. Is that weird?"

Sawyer froze. They did feel like his. Which was the opposite of what Maddie had been talking about. Shane and Max didn't feel like nephews. They felt like his *children*.

For a moment he couldn't move, couldn't breathe, couldn't think.

"You okay?" Cole asked. "'Cause you don't look it."

Sawyer wasn't sure *what* he was.

"And those four red ones with the big silver bows are for you, Max," Maddie said, pointing at the brightly wrapped gifts under the tree. "And Shane, those four silver ones with the red bows are yours. What could they be? I know—and you're both going to love everything, but you can't open them until Christmas. No peeking either."

Both babies were staring at the twinkling, beautiful tree from their carriers beside her. She was sitting cross-legged in front of the tree, rearranging the stacks of gifts that had grown today. She might have gone a little overboard in Mac-Leod's, where she insisted on paying and finally relented to an employee discount when her mother wouldn't hear of a Mac-Leod paying retail. She'd gotten cloth-ing and books and little stuffed animals for the boys, and then she'd done some shopping for her family in the wonderful shops on Main Street, buying her mom a pretty necklace and new fuzzy slippers she'd hinted she wanted, and for her sister a book on baby's first year and a gift cer-tificate to the Wedlock Creek Day Spa for a massage and mani-pedi. She'd gotten her dad the Irish fisherman sweater he'd been coveting from the L.L.Bean catalog, and she bought a big rawhide chew for Moose. For Cole she'd purchased a rug-ged watch with a cowboy on a horse on the center dial that she thought he'd like. All that was left on her list was Sawyer, and she was having a hard time coming up with a special gift for him. Luckily she still had a few days till Christmas Eve.

"Want to hear something crazy, boys?" she asked, turning to the babies. "I don't actually know if we open our gifts on Christmas Eve or on Christmas morning. No memory of that whatsoever. I'll have to ask Sawyer what our tradition is."

She heard his key in the lock and stood up, a baby carrier in each hand. Sawyer came in with Cole behind him, and unless it was her wishful imagination, both men looked relaxed and happy.

"Wow, something smells amazing," Cole said, sniffing the air. "What's for dinner?"

Maddie tried to keep the frown off her face. She'd expected Cole to rush over to the twins, marvel at their very being, ask how their day was. But Cole's first thought had been about how good the house smelled.

Was she being judgmental? Maybe. She slid a glance over at Sawyer, who was hanging up his and Cole's jackets. If he'd noticed, too, he didn't show it.

This is all new to Cole. Being here with the twins. Time with his brother. She'd been telling Sawyer to ease up; now she'd have to apply that to herself.

"I had a craving for pasta Bolognese and garlic bread," she said. She had to admit the house did smell delicious.

"I always have a craving for that," Cole said with a smile. He looked at the twins and gave a quick smile. "And here I thought babies cried all the time." He seemed fidgety and then sat down on the sofa. "They look so content."

Aw, he's just nervous, she realized. *These are his sons, and he doesn't feel connected to them because they've been here. This has to be really hard for him.*

She brought the carriers over to the sofa and put them down, taking out Max.

"This little guy was asking when you'd be over. He kept saying, 'Is it dinnertime yet?'"

Cole smiled and held out his arms. Maddie carefully transferred him. "When will they actually start talking? Six months?"

"More like around eighteen months—there's a big range. According to my mom, I said only five words until my second birthday, then I never shut up."

"Was one of those words *cake*?" Cole asked. "You're a cake fiend."

Cake... Maddie froze as a memory overtook her.

She was in the kitchen, but it was dark, and she'd opened the refrigerator to sneak a piece of the chocolate cake with incredible mocha icing from her birthday celebration earlier in the evening. She heard someone coming down the stairs quietly, as if trying not wake the house—

either Sawyer or Cole, since he'd asked to crash for a couple of days.

Moose was beside her, clearly hoping for a small bit of cake, which he was not going to get, and he hadn't alerted, so she assumed it was Sawyer, though Cole had paid him a lot of attention earlier, throwing ball after ball in the yard, so Moose likely thought of him as a family member now, despite Cole having not visited in a long time.

When Cole had heard it was her birthday, he'd run out before dinner and come back with two wrapped gifts in a Wedlock Creek Books shopping bag—a biography of Eleanor Roosevelt and a pretty blank journal with a matching fancy pen. She was so touched, and she'd written in the journal before turning in for the night earlier, about how glad she was that Cole was there and how she hoped this was the start of a new beginning for him and Sawyer.

She'd been about to open the fridge for her midnight snack of a sliver—okay, fine, a big slice—of cakewhen she heard a clinking sound coming from the living room.

Curious, she headed into the living room, the moonlight from the filmy living room curtains guiding her way. She was surprised to see Cole fully dressed, duffel over his shoulder. He stopped short of the living room doorway as he saw her standing there and his eyes widened.

"Sorry to surprise you—I had a cake craving." She glanced at his bag. "Don't tell me you're leaving?"

"Uh, yeah, I have to. I, uh, start a new job in the morning. I didn't want to jinx it by talking about it. You know how it is when you start a new job... You want to sleep in your own bed, have your stuff right there."

Was he lying? She couldn't tell. Some-

times she thought she knew Cole, and then sometimes she didn't.

"Well, I'm so happy you visited, Cole. It means a lot to Sawyer. Even if it doesn't show, trust me."

He seemed uncomfortable, shifting his feet. "It was good to see you, Maddie. I'm glad you liked your gifts." He started walking to the door.

"Let me go wake up Sawyer. He'll want to say goodbye."

"Nah, we have our systems," he said. "We're not goodbye types, you know?"

She smiled and hugged him. "You come back soon. And I want to hear all about the new job. Text me, okay?"

He gave her a quick smile, then rushed to the door. "Tell Sawyer sorry for me, okay?" She assumed he meant about leaving in the middle of the night without saying anything. Then he was out the door. The beater car roared to life and he peeled away.

Sawyer had come down immediately at the sound of the muffler. "Where's Cole going at one fifteen in the morning?"

"He said he had to leave, something about a new job starting tomorrow and wanting to sleep in his own bed. He said you two weren't much for goodbyes, and to tell you he was sorry."

"Sorry for what?"

Maddie shrugged. "Leaving when we thought he was going to stay another night?"

Sawyer's expression changed then. He went into the kitchen and turned on the light, then pulled off the top of the ceramic cookie jar in the shape of a bear on the counter. There weren't actually any cookies inside; it was where they kept their house cash.

She frowned. "Oh, Sawyer, really?" Why did he always think the worst of Cole?

He peered in and pulled out two twen-

ties and a ten-dollar bill. "How nice of him to leave us fifty bucks. Should I be impressed he didn't steal it all? There was over five hundred dollars in this, Maddie."

Her shoulders slumped, and she shook her head, tears coming to her eyes. "Sawyer, when I was in here before—I came down craving more birthday cake— I heard someone come downstairs and then a clinking sound in the living room. Then I went in and Cole looked startled and uncomfortable. Did he take something else?"

"Dammit." Sawyer stalked into the living room and turned on the lights, looking around.

"Oh no," she said, her gaze on the beautiful handmade wooden box with her name carved into it that her father had made for her several birthdays ago. "I keep my grandmother's bracelet in

there." The beautiful diamond tennis bracelet her nana had given her in hospice, two days before she passed. Tears stung Maddie's eyes, and she knew it was gone before Sawyer even rushed over to open the box.

"Just some silver earrings in here," he said, shaking his head. The look on Sawyer's face was one she rarely saw. Red-hot anger.

Tears fell down her cheeks and she made her way over to the sofa and cried. Sawyer sat beside her, taking her in his arms. Things had been so tense between her and her husband the past few months, and letting herself be held by him felt so good.

"He's not welcome here anymore, Maddie," Sawyer said. "No matter what. Final straw."

She nodded against his chest, crying, holding on to him.

* * *

"Maddie?" Sawyer said. "You look like you're a million miles away."

She started, realizing she'd been so lost in the memory that she'd disappeared for a while. She was standing in the same living room—just several months later. With Sawyer, staring at her with concern.

And Cole, whom she could never quite read.

"Sorry," she said. "Just thinking about something." She picked up Shane from his carrier and stroked his soft little cheek.

As she looked over at Cole, a cold snap ran up her spine. She went from trusting him to not trusting him, just like that. She thought Sawyer had been too hard on Cole? She'd been too hard on Sawyer.

Suddenly she understood why one of Sawyer's favorite phrases was *It's complicated*. It sure was.

"Cole impressed the hell out of me at the community center," Sawyer said.

"Heck, I mean," he added with a smile as he took Shane from Maddie and gave him a kiss on his downy head. *Let it go. If Sawyer is able to, just let it go.* Hadn't she been the one to say it's about now and the future?

Now and the future. She wondered just what was going to happen in the coming days. Or weeks. Or even months. Would Cole take back his sons?

And would Maddie say yes to her husband's offer of ten children because of the bargain he'd made when he'd been sitting by her hospital bedside, scared to death he'd lose her?

What she would give for a crystal ball for Christmas. One that actually worked.

Ugh, maybe scratch that, she thought. If she'd learned one thing from having lost her memory, it was that it was sometimes a good thing not to know too much. A blessing in disguise.

And anyway, things between the Wolfe

brothers seemed to change on a dime. Right now, they were in a good place. Did she really want to know if that was about to change?

Chapter Thirteen

"Whoa," Cole said, standing suddenly and scrunching up his face. "I think someone just went to the bathroom." He held his arms out as far as they would reach. "Maddie, can you take him?"

"Actually," she said with a smile, "why don't you change his diaper? No time like now to learn how."

"Uh, no, thanks," Cole said, giving his head a little shake to move his mop of wavy brown hair from his eyes. He gave

Maddie an imploring look. *Please take him—now.*

What? Did he just say no thanks about changing his son's diaper?

"Cole, it's one of the basics of parenthood," Maddie pointed out. "Changing diapers."

"I just haven't done it before. And to be honest, I don't want to." He grinned. "I mean, who would?"

Sawyer raised an eyebrow. "Cole, no one wants to change a dirty diaper. But you just do it. Like Maddie said, it's parenthood 101."

"Jeez, okay, fine," Cole said. "Kind of embarrassing to do it in front of people, though. Am I right?"

Sawyer gave a little roll of his eyes as he handed Shane to Maddie. "Let's go in the bathroom. There's a changing station. I'll show you the ropes."

"Great," Cole said so unenthusiastically that Maddie laughed.

Not that it was funny—at all. Cole would have to grow up. Then again, maybe they were just watching that in action. That was what family was. Taking the lumps with the great times. "Right, little guy?" she asked Max, nuzzling his cheek.

Five minutes later, Sawyer and Cole emerged from the bathroom, a triumphant look on Cole's face, Shane in his arms.

"That wasn't so bad," Cole said. "I mean, it was gross, but I got through it."

Maddie smiled. *Just wait till someone projectile vomits on you,* she thought. That had happened to her at MacLeod's one day—and when it wasn't your baby hurling all over you, it wasn't quite the same. It was much, much worse.

Wait a minute! She realized she'd just remembered that about MacLeod's. Not that she wanted to remember it. But it was another memory, a little one connected to something that had just happened as if she'd just plucked it right out of her head the way anyone accessed their thoughts. A jumble of memories followed, and she wasn't sure if it was the same time frame or not. She shook her head to clear it. Her memory was definitely on its way back.

"Should we feed them before we eat dinner?" Cole asked. "I like doing that. It's kind of fun."

Maddie smiled. "Actually, they ate right before you came. I tried to wait, but, oh boy, was Shane screeching his cute little head off to let me know they were starving."

"Oh, you know what?" Cole said, looking at his watch. "MacLeod's closes in fifteen minutes, right? I called this morning to order something for them, and your mom told me it would be ready tonight by closing. I got something personalized. I'd like to go pick it up and bring them back wearing what I got them. Your mom can help me change them into it."

Maddie caught Sawyer's hesitation, but then he said, "I'll have to install their car seats in your car. And don't speed."

"Bruh, I'm driving four blocks, and I'll park right out front."

Maddie glanced out the window. No snow today, so the roads were clear. How much trouble could he get into four blocks there, four blocks back? *Wait—don't answer that*, she told herself. "It was sweet of you to order them something. I can't wait to see what it is."

"Come on," Sawyer said. "I'll show you how to properly install the seats."

Maddie didn't love the idea of Cole driving them anywhere, even four blocks, but they needed to let him spend some time with the babies on his own. "I'll put them in their winter suits while you do that. You can lay Shane down in the bassinet till you're ready for the twins."

As the brothers walked into the foyer and put on their jackets, Cole said, "Maddie, I'm not ruining your spaghetti Bolognese, am I? I should be back in twenty minutes, tops."

"No problem," she said. It needs a good twenty minutes more. "And I wasn't going to put in the garlic bread for fifteen minutes anyway."

She took their fleece buntings from the closet and got the boys into them as Sawyer headed out with Cole. Then Maddie watched from the window as they installed the rear-facing car seats. She couldn't hear Sawyer giving Cole a lecture about the seats, but she was sure he was. They came back in, each taking a baby, and went back out. Maddie followed them and stayed on the porch, feeling a bit like her heart was about to be driven away. Sawyer joined her on the porch and put his arm around her.

"See you in twenty," Cole said as he

opened the driver's door. "Get your phones ready to take pics."

"Oh, wait, take their bag," Sawyer said. "Just in case. The bag always goes where they go. Just has some diapers, bottles, formula—basics if you're stuck in traffic, that kind of thing." Sawyer collected the stroller bag and handed it to Cole.

"Traffic on Main Street?" Cole said on a laugh, putting the bag in the front seat. "That's my bro, always prepared," he added to Maddie with a roll of his eyes.

That's a good thing, Cole.

They watched the noisy black car drive very slowly up to Main Street.

Sawyer smiled. "I could actually ticket him for going *that* slow."

"Makes me feel better to see him inching down the street." She turned to Sawyer and squeezed his hand, then went inside, Sawyer following. "By the way, I remembered the theft. When Cole mentioned the word *cake* before, the entire incident unlocked in my head. Happy birthday, me."

"Yeah, I didn't want to mention that added zinger when I brought it up. But it made it a lot worse for me."

"You had a good day with him. I'm glad."

"Me too. And…" He trailed off as if suddenly shy about something, and Sawyer Wolfe wasn't typically reticent with what was on his mind.

"And what?" she asked, slipping her arms around his neck.

He looked at her, putting his hands on either side of her face. He kissed her, and she felt her knees wobble. With love. With desire. With everything that had come before and everything that was to come. She loved this man.

"And I felt something shift in me, Maddie. Just a little. But something happened tonight at the community center, watching Cole with Jake, the way the two of us were talking, really talking. I felt something give way, loosen up."

Wait—was he saying what she thought he was saying? Was he ready to start a family—and not because of the bargain?

As if he could read her mind, he added, "I'm not saying I'm completely over the hump. But something feels a little different inside."

She squeezed him into a hug and held him tight, resting her head on his chest and hopefully saying more than she could manage right now. He had to know how much that meant to her—even to the Maddie she was with one-eighth of her memories. She'd take that *little different inside*. It was very likely more than Maddie-with-*all*-her-memories had ever gotten from Sawyer. It was a beautiful start.

We're on our way, she thought.

"I'll go make the garlic bread," he said, and she could tell he was feeling vulnerable and needed some space with what he felt, what he'd admitted, the newness of it all.

She glanced at the clock. "Yeah, timing seems right. He should be back in ten minutes."

As Sawyer went into the kitchen, she missed him immediately. She missed the twins too. Felt strange to be in the house with Sawyer yet without Max and Shane.

Maddie spent those ten minutes appreciating the delicious aroma of garlic bread baking in the oven and having absolutely nothing to do but anticipate eating it and the Bolognese. She didn't have to be on red alert for a crying baby or diaper duty or feed a little being. She stretched out on the couch and put her feet up on the coffee table. She'd absolutely loved being a mom to the twins this past week, but it was also nice to do nothing at all.

"I stirred the sauce," Sawyer said as he

came into the room. He looked up at the big wall clock. "Garlic bread's on warm right now, but if he's not back in five minutes, we'll have to gobble it up ourselves to save it."

Maddie smiled. "I'm sure he'll be back any minute."

Except he wasn't. Not five minutes later. Or ten.

He should have been back twenty minutes ago.

Sawyer grabbed his phone. He called the store. "April, it's Sawyer. Has my brother been in?" Maddie watched him listen. "Oh, good. Yeah, that does sound very cute. Great. Thanks." He clicked his phone off. "Your mom said Cole came in with the twins and she helped him change them into their new personalized pajamas, their names across the front. He left about five minutes ago."

So why wasn't he back? Now it was five

minutes after that. Then ten minutes. It was a forty-second drive from their house to MacLeod's.

Sawyer was staring at his phone. "I just texted him. No response."

Maddie grabbed her own phone and called him. "He's not picking up. Because he's driving? Maybe his car doesn't have Bluetooth?"

"It does."

Maddie's stomach twisted. "Why isn't he back?" She heard the wobble in her voice.

He grabbed his phone again and pressed in a number. "Hey, Mobley. Do me a favor and look around for a small black Chevy, muffler on the fritz." He read off the license plate. "My brother was supposed to be back a half hour ago, and I'm worried he may have gotten into an accident. Any calls come in?"

"Nope, not in the past hour. Although I did see—and hear—a very noisy little black Chevy pass me on Main Street twenty minutes ago. It was headed toward the service road, not your house, though."

A chill ran up Sawyer's spine.

"Should I go looking for him?" Mobley asked.

"I've got it. Thanks, though," he said. He pocketed his phone, his expression grim.

"What's going on?" Maddie asked.

He closed his eyes for a second. "My rookie saw Cole driving south on Main Street twenty minutes ago. Headed out of town."

"What? Why?" The panic in her voice scared her even more than she was already.

"I'm going after him," he said, grabbing his leather jacket.

"I'm coming. It's not like there are babies here requiring me to stay."

She thought she felt a chill before?

* * *

What the hell, Cole? Sawyer thought as he headed to the Johannsen ranch, which was about fifteen minutes from town. The ranch—Cole's home now—seemed the likeliest place to start to look for his brother and the twins.

"He'll be there, right?" Maddie asked, worry in her blue eyes.

"I can't imagine where else he could go."

Maddie nodded. "He'll be there. Why didn't he just come back to our house? Why'd he take off?"

"We're going to have to get that answer from Cole. I just don't know."

They drove the rest of the way in silence, Maddie staring grimly out the window, Sawyer holding the steering wheel a little too tightly. Finally, they approached the sign for the Johannsen ranch and drove up the quarter-mile dirt road until a weathered gray farmhouse and two barns came into view. There was no sign of the little black car.

The border collie Cole had been telling Jake about at the community center came running toward the car to greet them. "Hey, boy," he said, giving the dog a pat as he got out. "Have you seen my brother?"

"Dog doesn't talk, so you'd better ask me," a grizzled voice said.

Abe Johannsen came off the porch and down the three steps. Sawyer had known Abe a long time; he was a fixture in town, particularly at Dee's Diner every morning at six for breakfast. His son, Joe, ran the ranch with a cowboy or two over the years, and now that cowboy was Cole. "Chief. You say you're looking for your brother?"

Sawyer met him near the base of the steps. "Nice to see you, Abe. Yes, I'm looking for Cole. Works for you, right?" Unless Cole was lying about that.

"Sure does. Hard worker too. He impressed Joe the past two days, and Joe's a tough one to impress. Of course, we only gave him the job because we knew he was your brother."

Okay by him. And he was relieved to hear Cole was working out here. Joe was a serious dude, married to an equally serious wife named Lauren, so Cole had to be bringing his A game to impress them. Their own kids, twins, had graduated from high school the year before and had enlisted in the army, if Sawyer remembered correctly.

"Glad to hear it," Sawyer said. "Is he here?"

Abe nodded. "Heard that mess of a car pull in about forty minutes ago. Over dinner Lauren said she might just have to front Cole a car so she doesn't have to listen to that muffler. If you drive down that way two minutes, you'll come to his cabin. Oh, and say hello to Maddie for me." He gave a wave toward the car, and Maddie waved back, though she likely didn't remember Abe.

Sawyer said he would and thanked him and got back into the car, where Maddie was waiting. He reiterated what Abe had said, and the relief on her face was something to behold. He drove the two minutes and saw Cole's car, then the cabin, small, rustic and dark brown. The evergreen out front was encircled with white lights, and he wondered if Cole had done that or if Abe had.

Sawyer and Maddie walked up the two porch steps to the landing. A small wreath was hanging on the front door. Another nice touch. Sawyer knocked, then found himself holding his breath.

No answer.

Sawyer knocked again. "I know you're in there, Cole."

Footsteps sounded, and the door opened. Cole stood there, looking a bit shell-shocked. As if he couldn't believe what he'd done and was now just realizing it. Good. Sawyer and Maddie would take the twins and go home.

"It's really cold out," Maddie said to Cole. "Can we come in?"

"Oh, uh, sure." Cole opened the door wide.

The twins were in the car seats at the edge of a big oval braided rug in the main room, one asleep, the other fighting sleep and losing. Sawyer caught Shane's eyes close and stay closed.

"I have everything under control, as you see," Cole said. "So if you were worried about my sons, they're fine."

My sons. Had Cole actually used that phrasing before?

"So last we heard, you were going to MacLeod's and would be back in twenty minutes," Sawyer prompted.

Cole bit his lip. "I took them to MacLeod's and it was a madhouse—really crowded. All these women were coming up to me and the twins and saying how adorable they were and asking their names and saying how proud I must be, and I was like, I am proud. I didn't really think about that before. I *am* proud to be their dad."

Where the hell was this going? Nowhere good.

He's their father, he reminded himself, so many emotions slamming into him he couldn't tell them apart.

Maddie moved over to the tan sofa and sat down. She patted the seat beside her, and Sawyer sat too. He knew his wife, and she was telling him not to be combative. "You should definitely be proud, Cole."

He gave her something of a smile and sat in the chair across from the sofa. "Maddie, your mom helped me change them into their new pajamas with their names, and when I saw the twins wearing them, something just connected inside me. I can't fully explain it. It's like all synapses finally fired or something."

Sawyer could explain it. It was what he'd felt at the community center when he and Cole and Jake were together. The shift inside him—something big and previously unmovable had budged. Just a little for him, but it had. Now Cole had experienced that same thing.

Which meant what, exactly?

"Maddie and I are happy to raise the twins," Sawyer said. "I just want you to know that before we go any further here. We love these boys like they're our own. If you're not up to being a father, full speed ahead, full commitment, we'll take them home right now."

Cole glared at him. "If you want a baby so bad, Sawyer, have one."

Sawyer felt the blood rush from his face. He glanced at Maddie, who had a million emotions on her face. "This isn't about me. It's about you and the twins."

"Stop calling them the twins and start calling them my sons. That's what they are. Mine. Shane and Max are my sons and they should be with me. I should be raising them."

"You should be raising them if you're in a position to do that," Sawyer said.

"I'll make it my position," Cole snapped. "I've been thinking about this. A lot. Yeah, I've got a lot to learn. But I'll learn it. Just like I learned to change a diaper tonight. I'm not abandoning my kids the way my dad abandoned me."

Ah. There it was. What this was really about. Sawyer had no doubt that Cole wanted to raise his children—because he knew what was it was like to be cast aside. But Sawyer did doubt that Cole had the necessary tools right now for the job.

"Cole, I understand what you're saying," Maddie said. "And you should be commended. You *are* their father. But I also hear what Sawyer's saying—for one, you work full-time."

Cole crossed his arms over his chest. "So do a lot of other working parents. You've heard of nannies?"

"On your salary?" Sawyer asked.

"I'll make do. I'll figure something out. There are day cares too. I think they're supposed to be less expensive." He turned to Maddie. "Don't even think about saying you'll be the nanny for free, because I won't take advantage of you like that. I've done enough of that already."

That surprised Sawyer. He stared at Cole, once again unsure what the hell to make of this. Part of what Cole was saying was right. Yes, he should raise his kids. Yes, single working parents managed every day.

But the part that was wrong had to do with Cole—and who he was right now. Could he surprise Sawyer and become a decent parent? Maybe with a question mark? If he really tried? But Sawyer was going to be very honest with himself and say not in the near future.

"So you plan to be a full-time father," Sawyer said. "Do you really understand how much your life is going to change? Starting right now, Cole."

Cole lifted his chin. "Yes, I do."

Sawyer looked at Maddie, who seemed to be trying to hide the same worry as he was. This felt too fast, too impulsive on Cole's part. But it wasn't like Sawyer could pick up the twins and leave with them and say, *That's all nice to hear, but we'll take them home. Come visit anytime.*

As his brother had pointed out, Cole was the father here. Not Sawyer.

Sawyer stared at the twins, both asleep, so peaceful, so beautiful. He wanted to rush over and scoop them up and run. But they weren't his. And he couldn't.

He cleared his throat, his chest all tight. "Well, then. We're fifteen minutes away if you ever need help, Cole. We're both here for you and the twins. You know that, right?"

Cole's expression softened. "Yeah, I know. I've got this. And they're easy babies. You said so yourselves."

Maddie slid a glance at him. Cole had no idea. But there was only one way for him to find out.

It's like you want him to fail, Sawyer thought, shame creeping in. That wasn't fair to Cole. Or the twins.

"Since I gave you their bag," Sawyer said, "you have what they need for the night. But stop by in the morning or your lunch break and you can pick up some of their other things. The bassinets, their favorite lullaby player, clothes."

"I'll do that," Cole said.

Maddie looked like she might burst into tears. He needed to get her out of here, but the thought of leaving Shane and Max here was almost unbearable.

"Make sure to wash their bottles out well. And the nipples too," she said. "And use ointment if you see redness or chafing during diaper changes."

Cole grimaced. "I will. I bought a book on twins' first year from MacLeod's. Actually, your mom wouldn't let me pay. For their personalized pajamas either."

"Yeah, my mom's like that," she said. "You're family."

Surprise lit Cole's eyes, and he gave her a smile.

A cry came from behind them, and Maddie popped up, then sat back down. They were off-duty from here on in.

"Well, fatherhood calls," Cole said, standing and turning toward his sons.

Sawyer sure hoped so. For the sake of two newborns Sawyer loved very much.

He and Maddie stood and inched toward the door, both of them watching

Cole pick up Max and cradle him against his chest. So far, so good.

But getting himself to actually walk out the door of this little cabin and leave his heart in those carriers was another story.

"I'll be fine," Cole said. "Really. I'm a grown-up."

Sawyer nodded. "Well, like I said, you need anything, we're here for you."

"Anything," Maddie said. "Text or call anytime, day or night."

"Honestly, you two can go now," Cole said, impatience in his tone. "I think Max wants to hear the book I got him today."

Maddie linked arms with Sawyer, almost hanging on him as if she needed the help physically walking out the door. But they did leave.

When they got outside, the door closing behind him, Maddie staggered a bit, almost like she had too much to drink. But she'd barely had a half cup of eggnog a couple hours ago.

"Maddie?"

She didn't say anything.

"Maddie?" he repeated.

She hung on to him harder, as though her knees would buckle if she didn't.

She was not okay. At all. He was upset about the twins, too, but Maddie was clearly taking it even harder. Although as he looked at her, she seemed *physically* ill right now.

"Help me to the car," she barely managed to say.

He opened her door and got her inside, then closed the door and ran around to the driver's side, sliding in.

Then all hell broke loose.

Chapter Fourteen

Maddie couldn't stop shaking. But when she looked at her hands, they weren't even trembling. Or were they?

She closed her eyes, dimly aware of Sawyer calling her name.

"I'm going to call 911," he said, reaching for his phone.

"You hate pickles," she said, wonder on her face. "Your father broke his ankle, and one of his many fiancées broke up with him because he'd need too much help. MacLeod's did even better this year than last year, and that's saying some-thing."

He stared at her, his jaw dropping open slightly. "Maddie? Your memory is com-pletely back?"

Tears filled her eyes and she nodded five times. "I remember! I remember! Oh God, Sawyer, it's all back!"

He let out one hell of a deep breath. "You scared me to death." He wrapped his arms around her best he could with a console between them. "My Maddie is back."

He had no doubt the stress of leaving Max and Shane in that little cabin with Cole had shocked her system.

"I'm back!" she said, laughing and cry-ing at the same time. "I know my life again! What you've been through this week, Sawyer. Wow."

"I'm not the one who got into a car accident and lost my memory," he re-minded her.

"I was in blissful ignorance, though. You, on the other hand, faced just about every one of your deepest fears. Head-on. And came out stronger."

He stared at her. "What are you talking about?"

"How impossible are you—*still*?" she said, her eyes twinkling. "The babies. Your brother. All of it."

But his expression told her he didn't feel stronger. That, in fact, he might be feeling the opposite. And his least favorite adjective when it came to himself: *powerless*.

She reached for his hand. "Sawyer, I know that leaving the twins with Cole feels wrong. No matter what he professes or wants to believe about himself. But we have to give him a chance. For one, we don't have a choice. For another, we need to have faith."

"You *are* back," he said, putting his hands on either side of her face and kissing her. Gently. Then more passionately.

"I have so much to say, too much. But all I want to say is that I love you."

"I love you, too, Maddie. You know that, right? Above everything else?"

She nodded. "I know."

The sound of a baby crying—Shane, if she wasn't mistaken—pierced the quiet of the ranch, and they both turned toward the cabin, where Cole paced back and forth, an infant in his arms.

"Maybe we can just live in the car, in this clearing," he said, eyeing the windows, "so we can keep watch."

She smiled. "Well, at least we know he's doing what he's supposed to. I think we can leave feeling okay about this. Let's give him a chance," she repeated. "And go home."

If you want a baby so bad, Sawyer, have one.

If she ever lost her memory again, she had no doubt in her mind that she'd never forget the look on Sawyer's face as Cole had said that.

Sawyer had seemed shocked, but she knew him too well. He'd been *surprised*. He'd said something had shifted inside him while he'd been volunteering at the community center and Cole had joined them, that the immovable had budged. And the surprise on his face told her that something had budged just a little more.

She felt more hopeful than she ever had.

In the morning, Sawyer expected a "we're fine, stop worrying text" from Cole, but none came. Which of course likely meant they were fine. But he couldn't stop worrying. Although, granted, it was barely seven.

But didn't cowboy Cole get up with the cows and chickens? Would he be working today? Who'd watch the twins? Grizzled old Abe? That wouldn't be happening. Joe or Lauren? Maybe. But he couldn't see it.

The twins were alone in the cabin. Screaming. Hungry. Wet. They'd be all alone all day.

Sawyer started pacing in his study, trying to tell himself that was not the case. But it could be. Cole wasn't exactly full of common sense. Maybe he thought he could leave the twins for a few hours and that they'd nap the whole time.

Where was the roll of Tums? He rummaged through his desk drawer in need of antacids, popped two and dropped down onto his desk chair. Moose eyed him and came over, putting his chin on Sawyer's thigh.

"Good dog," Sawyer said, petting his majestic head.

He heard footsteps upstairs—Maddie was awake. When they'd gotten home last night, she'd called Dr. Addison's service to leave a message reporting that her memory had returned, and the doctor had called her back almost immediately. She'd told Maddie to expect to be tired that night and not to fight it, that she needed a very good night's rest.

"See, it's almost a good thing Shane and Max aren't here to wake me up three times during the night," she'd said—gently.

If you want a baby so bad, Sawyer, have one.

All night, as Maddie slept beside him, he kept replaying that over and over in his head.

But instead of *Okay, I think I will* as his answer, he just felt mired in quicksand. Because he'd left his heart in that cabin and every old bad feeling about being unable to do what he wanted, what he needed, came rushing over him.

He couldn't control his father and make him act the way he should.

He couldn't control Cole and make him act the way he should.

Cripes. It was exactly how Maddie

must feel about him. *I can't control Sawyer and make him act the way he should.*

He froze. *That* was what he was doing to his beloved wife?

He closed his eyes and leaned his head back, then snapped to attention. He couldn't sit here and get sucked down into that quicksand anymore. He needed to act. He needed to know the twins weren't alone in the cabin, crying their eyes out with full diapers. And hungry.

He took the stairs two at a time and found Maddie emerging from the shower, her pretty long brown hair damp past her shoulders. He was full of vinegar, but for a moment, everything faded, and all he saw was her—his beautiful wife. His *everything.*

"I thought I'd bring some stuff for the twins over to the cabin," he said. "Want to come?"

"You're so transparent, Sawyer Wolfe," she said. "You want to check on Max and

Shane. You're envisioning them all alone, aren't you?"

"Guilty. And unfortunately, it's not so far-fetched."

Her smiled faded. "No, I guess not. But I'm sure they're fine. He's either taken the day off or he asked someone to stay with them."

"Eighty-seven-year-old Abe?" Sawyer said, raising an eyebrow.

"Abe is sharp as a tack," she pointed out. "He finishes the crossword puzzle in Dee's Diner every morning before anyone else at the counter. Dee told me that herself. Maybe he skipped this morning at the diner to babysit."

"Sharp and 'wants to babysit' are worlds apart, Maddie."

She laughed. "Let's go load the SUV."

Turned out that Max and Shane had not been crying and hungry and all alone in the cabin. Joe and Lauren had offered to babysit the twins in their house for a few days until Cole could line up a nanny. They also gave him a raise. The Johannsens had both sung Cole's praises— that he was twice the worker their last hand was, that he was exceptionally strong for a lanky guy and that he was polite, particularly to the people coming to the ranch to drop off this or that.

Sawyer and Maddie had been invited into the farmhouse and to say hello to their nephews. Joe and Lauren were actually thrilled to have the little guests for a few days. Joe had played peekaboo at least ten times with the twins, and Lauren had gone from the super-serious person he'd remembered to listening to an impressive bout of baby talk and watching her cuddle each baby.

Boy, did Sawyer feel better.

"I'm so glad you suggested bringing things over," Maddie said as they drove back toward town. "I feel so much better now. This just might work out."

"You know, it just might. Cole can be capable of good surprises too. I often forget that."

Because when it mattered, Cole had taken care of business. He'd gotten a solid job with room and board. He'd found trustworthy people—his bosses—to watch the twins while he worked. He had likely put out feelers for a nanny. Especially because he could now afford to pay for said nanny.

Maybe Sawyer would go over in the next couple of days and he and Cole could look at the cabin with an eye toward sectioning off a nursery with a room divider. Maddie was the interior decorator among them, and she'd do wonders with the place to turn it from cowboy cabin to cozy family home.

"I need to ask you something," Maddie said as he turned onto Main Street. He parked in the public lot near the chapel, since they planned on doing their final shopping for their Holiday Happymakers recipients.

"I'm listening," he said, turning to face her.

"I wasn't going to push with this. But given all that's happened, Sawyer, I do want to know where things stand. Are we having ten children? Or are we starting with one—maybe two at the same time, since twins do run in the family, and we did marry at this chapel with its legend of the multiples."

He knew what she was asking—if he was ready to be a father. And not because of the bargain he'd made. But because he wanted to be.

He reached into his pocket for the roll of Tums, but then realized he'd hurt Maddie's feelings if he ate one, let alone the entire roll, which he needed right now. He wasn't really ready for this question.

But it had been the question for their entire lives, not just during their marriage. Not just this past difficult year.

Sawyer looked up at the chapel, just in time to see Champ, the beagle mascot, grab half a bagel slathered in cream cheese off the sidewalk that a man had accidentally dropped. He smiled to himself, glad he could smile right now. *That's the way, Champ. Go for the stuff that people drop instead of stealing.*

He'd have to talk to Annie Potterowski again about Champ being out loose on chapel grounds. Had he not told her to keep Champ on a short leash?

Yeah, keep thinking about the beagle right now instead of the important question your wife just asked you.

"Sawyer?"

He cleared his throat. "I just feel so up in the air right now. About Cole. Things seem okay, but it's been one day."

"We need to let Cole be. And please

stop making excuses, Sawyer Wolfe. I want to know if your feelings have changed about starting a family."

He turned toward her. "I promised you ten kids if that's how many you want, Mads. So yes, let's start a family." Should he feel joyful that he was saying yes and giving her what she wanted? All he felt was that he was being pulled down further into the quicksand.

If you want a baby so bad, Sawyer, have one.

Why was this so hard for him? He loved Shane and Max. Loved caring for them, having them in his house. So why was he still so…scared? That was the word for it. Not a word the chief of police would ever want applied to him.

Her face fell, and she stared straight ahead. "So nothing has changed. You bargained for my life, the universe came through and now you're making good on your end of the deal. Great. I get the family I want with a husband who really doesn't want his own children." She opened the door and got out, hurrying toward the sidewalk.

No, no, no. This was not happening. Again. Panic clawed at him, and he got out of the SUV and chased after her, but she was gone. It was now just past nine and the shops were all open and bustling with last-minute shoppers the day before Christmas Eve. He peered into a few store windows, but he didn't see her.

He pulled out his phone and texted her. Maddie, let's talk. Please.

Not right now, she texted back.

His heart so heavy he was surprised he didn't drop to the ground, Sawyer went into the grocery store and ordered a ham for his Holiday Happymakers family's wish list, then bought a $250 gift card to the store. He stopped in MacLeod's, hoping to see Maddie, but she wasn't there, and April and Jenna were both very busy with customers. He bought pajamas for the baby as the mother on the form had requested, then stopped at the toy store for the toddler's yellow dump truck, then stopped into the gift shop for the wool socks for the dad with the Wedlock Creek logo on it. He bought ten pairs of those. He added another gift card, dropped it all in a red holiday bag and brought it over to the community center.

A woman behind the desk had a big smile on her face as he handed over the bag and the ticket from his envelope, explaining about the ham. She said she'd call the family today and let them know they could pick up their ham anytime today and she'd deliver their bag of gifts herself.

Now it was time to go buy Jake's bike. There was one bike shop in town, a big store at the far end of Main Street, and the place did amazing business given all the kids in town—and the multiples. Sawyer looked around the crowded shop, and there it was. The bike of Jake Russtower's nine-year-old dreams.

A silver mountain bike with orange stripes. He had the salesclerk add a water-bottle holder and a rack for Jake's backpack. He also bought a silver helmet. He was about to bring both over to the community center, then wondered if Cole would be volunteering tonight. How could he, though? He could bring the twins, and Sawyer could watch them while Cole volunteered. He thought about Jake being disappointed if his new superhero didn't show up, and he texted Cole.

Volunteering with me tonight at the community center? I know Jake will want to see you, so I'd be happy to hang with the twins on the bleachers for even just a half hour while you connect with Jake. Oh, and I got his bike and a cool helmet. Maybe I'll give it to him there.

Cole texted back.

I'll take you up on that offer to watch the twins while I volunteer. Oh, and you should give the bike to his dad and let his dad give Jake the bike for Christmas.

Sawyer sat back in his SUV, stunned.

Yes, that was *exactly* what he should do. Whether Vince Russtower deserved that or not—*Jake* did.

You're absolutely right, Cole. I owe you one. Didn't even think of that.

See, I'm not so bad—all the time.

Tears stung Sawyer's eyes, and he blinked them back hard. Hadn't he just said that Cole was full of surprises? He sure as hell was.

Sawyer shook his head to get hold of himself and figured he'd do an online search for Vince Russtower's number. He could probably get it from Reed Barelli's registration list from the baby-rearing class he'd taught. He was about to drive toward the PD when he saw Vince Russtower standing on Main Street. He was alone, looking in the window of Wedlock Creek Toys. That was a lucky break. But then again, it seemed the entire town was out this morning.

He approached Vince, who seemed to be looking at a remote-control helicopter in the window. Only $39.99! Holiday special! the little sign beside it said. "Hey, Vince."

The guy turned, his chin lifting as he regarded Sawyer. "My son Jake never stops talking about you and your brother."

"All good things, I hope," Sawyer said.

"A little hero worship." Vince turned back toward the helicopter. "He used to make me feel like I was his hero, but since I got married and had the baby, we haven't had as much time for each other."

"Maybe you could hang with Jake at the center even just one night a week, show up an hour early to pick him up."

"I'm actually going to be doing that every Monday and Friday from now on," he said. "Amy—my wife—suggested that. She said Jake talked to her about wanting to spend more time with me."

Whoa. Score another gold point for Cole—and Jake for following through.

"Dammit, I wish I had the money for that copter," Vince said, staring at it. "Jake would love that. But we're on a really tight budget. I got him a book he wanted and some temporary tattoos I know he'll love." The disappointment on Vince's face was heartbreaking.

"Did you know that Jake filled out a gift request on the Holiday Happymakers tree? He asked for a bike. And I happened to get the request. Bike's in my car. Helmet too."

Vince's eyes widened. "Wow. You bought him a bike?"

"My brother and I think it would mean more if it came from you—if it's *your* Christmas present to him. You be Santa."

Vince stared at him. "Why would you do that for me?" He looked down at the ground, and Sawyer knew what he was thinking: *Why would you do that for me when I stole from the multiples class—a class I got a free pass to because I had only one baby and made a stink about discrimination against single kids?*

Sawyer smiled inwardly about that. Detective Barelli had had a soft spot for Russtower since he knew him from summer camp or something like that. Sawyer hadn't been that generous or gracious. And he'd always believed Russtower had stolen the bottles and blanket. But right now, everything seemed to be about second chances. Vince seemed different to Sawyer, though it had barely been six months since that incident. The guy seemed more grounded.

"Because it's Christmas," Sawyer said. "And because you pick up Jake at the center every night and sling his backpack over your shoulder. You're there for him, Vince. Maybe not as much as he'd like, but you do have a new baby. You give him that bike. It *is* from you." Sawyer extended his hand, and Vince shook it.

"I don't know what else to say but thank you. I won't ever forget this."

A few minutes later, the bike and helmet were in Vince Russtower's car.

And something else had been transferred—to no one. Something big and heavy. Something that had been pulling him in and under.

He let out a deep breath and walked along Main Street, thinking about what he could get Maddie. It had to be something very special, like she was.

An hour later, all he had was a gold

heart locket on a delicate chain that he knew she'd love. The locket opened, and she could put tiny photos of her nephews on one side and photos of her sister's babies when they arrived in February. The locket was nice, but it wasn't enough.

He walked up and down the sidewalk on both sides of Main Street, peering into stores, looking through racks and displays. And the more he tried to think of the perfect gift for his wife, the more he realized something else, something he rushed back home to tell her.

Maddie put on the Woodstock earrings Sawyer had given her for her Christmas when they were sixteen. They were incredibly goofy, but the tiny yellow Woodstocks were wearing a green-and-red Christmas sweater, and they'd always made her smile.

She needed to smile.

She'd spent the past few hours at home—thinking. And realizing that the greatest gift she could give Sawyer was to let him be who he was. To her, he was a born father, daddy of the year. But for all his reasons, he didn't want to be.

What Maddie had finally realized was that she loved Sawyer Wolfe totally and fully and always had, and Sawyer Wolfe had never wanted kids. He'd known this, stated this, never veered from this his entire life. She'd been telling herself this for seven years, but she'd never *accepted* it.

She would be one hell of an aunt. To Shane and Max. To her sister's twins. She'd babysit a lot. She'd resume volunteering with the newborns at the hospital in Brewer. And she'd do all that without bitterness, without resentment. Because what she wanted more than anything, what she'd always wanted more than anything, was Sawyer. She understood that now in a way she hadn't before.

She wouldn't be a mom. But her life would be full and rich and happy regardless.

Okay, fine, it would take more than one morning to fully accept that she was letting go of a dream. But she was at peace with her decision.

She heard Sawyer's key in the door, a sound she wanted to hear for the rest of her life. Her husband coming home.

"I have something for you," he said, holding up a shopping bag from Mac-Leod's. "Luckily the store was so crowded that your mom and sister didn't even see me. I was able to buy this at the register with a salesclerk who didn't recognize me."

She tilted her head. "Why would it be a secret?"

"Because the first person I want to know about it is you."

"What is it?"

"Oh, wait, before I forget, let me put

your Christmas present under the tree," he said, taking a small package from his pocket and walking into the living room. He knelt down and put the little gift on top of one of the twins' presents.

She followed him to the tree. "So this—from MacLeod's—isn't my Christmas present?" she asked.

"Nope. It's more an everyday present." He reached into the bag and pulled out a large wrapped box and handed it to her.

She gave it a little shake. "What could you possibly have gotten me from Mac-Leod's Multiples Emporium?"

Moose watching from his dog bed by the fireplace, she ripped open the paper, then took off the top of the box.

A drapey off-white fuzzy sweater be-dazzled with Mommy to Be across the chest.

She stared at it, then looked at Sawyer. "I'm confused."

"It's a maternity sweater. When I brought

it to the counter to pay, the salesclerk said she bought her sister one, and it still fits her even though she's nine months now."

"I repeat—I'm confused," Maddie said.

He took her face in his hands and looked straight into her eyes. "I've been scared, Maddie. I didn't realize *that* was the word for what was keeping me blocked about children until this morning. I always thought it was something else. A lot of something else. But it's just pure *fear*."

Hope stirred in Maddie's heart. She looked at the sweater in her hands, and tears filled her eyes. "Are you saying…"

"I'm saying I'm sorry I denied you your dream of being a mom for so long. I'm sorry I've let you down. I want to start a family, Maddie. Right now. And I don't want ten children. I just want one to start. Twins would be just fine."

She put the sweater onto the console table and threw her arm around him. "I was going to tell you that I'm okay with not having kids. That all I've ever truly wanted was you."

"I want to be a father. I think I'm actually meant to be a father. And we already both know you're meant to be a mother."

Sawyer's phone pinged. Text from Cole.

We're invited for Christmas, right?

Sawyer held up the phone to Maddie, then texted back.

You three had better come. We might have gone overboard on gifts for our nephews.

Feel free to keep doing that for the rest of their lives. Good news—I hired a nanny. We went to high school together—I had a huge crush on her. Her dad's a cop for the WCPD—Mike Bauer. You probably met Bea a million times.

Sawyer envisioned a petite, talkative redhead in her twenties with big green eyes. A little girl had gotten separated from her parents at the multiples fair last summer, and Mike Bauer's daughter had been dropping something off for her dad and comforted the girl until her parents' came, drawing pictures with her.

Sawyer texted: Sounds great. Invite her to stop by Christmas Eve.

I already did, he texted back with a laughing emoji.

Sawyer smiled and pocketed his phone. "This is going to be our best Christmas ever," he said to his wife.

Maddie kissed him. "Yup. Let's go start that family right now."

He picked her up and carried her up the stairs, Christmas wishes they hadn't even known they had all coming true.

* * * * *

LET'S TALK

Romance

For exclusive extracts, competitions
and special offers, find us online:

f facebook.com/millsandboon

⊙ @millsandboonuk

🐦 @millsandboon

Or get in touch on 0844 844 1351*

For all the latest titles coming soon,
visit millsandboon.co.uk/nextmonth

Want even more
ROMANCE?

Join our bookclub today!

'Mills & Boon books, the perfect way to escape for an hour or so.'

Miss W. Dyer

'Excellent service, promptly delivered and very good subscription choices.'

Miss A. Pearson

'You get fantastic special offers and the chance to get books before they hit the shops'

Mrs V. Hall

Visit millsandbook.co.uk/Bookclub and save on brand new books.

MILLS & BOON